The Greek Constellations - Pandora

The Greek Constellations - Pandora

Stephan De Jonghe

The Greek Constellations – Pandora

The Greek Constellations – Pandora, by Stephan De Jonghe
International
ISBN 978-0-6453718-6-4 (paperback)
ISBN 978-0-6453718-7-1 (e-book)
USA
ISBN 0-6453718-6-6 (paperback)
ISBN 0-6453718-7-4 (e-book)

Publisher Stephan De Jonghe Publishing,
Hillarys, Perth, Western Australia, Australia 6025

For permission requests, write to
the publisher at: stephansfolliclefarm@gmail.com

Ordering Information:
Special discounts are available on quantity purchases by book re-sellers, corporations, associations, and others.
For details, contact the publisher at the email address above.

Cover

In the footsteps of Homer and Hesiod.

From astronomy to mythology

How the constellations came to be named by the Greek God's.

Stephan De Jonghe

Novella Three

Saturn's moon

Pandora: the story of the first human woman

The dedication

To say that my darling wife is the love of my life is
an understatement.

Deb is my best friend, soul mate, confidant, and life partner.
Among so many other things, we also share a love of books, and
we have a massive library on display in our home of books that we
want to read.

Our topics include action, comedy, romance, science fiction,
crime, thrillers, and adventure. We also have
an impressive non-fiction collection.

My endeavours as an author represent a passion that burns pow-
erfully for me. I am driven to write.
I have many stories to tell, and writing them and publishing them
is my way of contributing to other people's library's.

Writing involves many hours of research and then sitting in soli-
tude,
slowly assembling the words that details a journey into a readable
story.
One that was only previously an idea.

This takes a lot of patience and persistence.
After the story is put down, the process of editing begins.
Few non-writers understand that this stage can take as much as
five times longer than it takes to write the actual first draft.

My Deb gives me the support that I need
to execute my writing passion.
She not only supports my writing,
but she also enjoys reading the stories.

Her assistance with proof reading, feed-back on content,
and editing, is invaluable.
Especially after I've become blind to my own errors.
She understands how important it is to me
and to you, the reader, to get it right.

I dedicate these books to my wife as my thanks
to her for her ongoing support,
and for her contributions to the finished publications.

We are a team.

We both hope that you enjoy this series of books,
and we look forward to your feedback.

Stephan and Deb De Jonghe

Special thanks

My special thanks go to Janey Emery – Renowned Australian artist, for giving me permission to use her art for the covers for my Greek Constellation series of books.

I hope you enjoy her art and the story within these pages.

Stephan De Jonghe - Author

Janey's Story - Born in Narrogin, Western Australia, Janey Emery's interest in art began as early as 2 years of age and led to art becoming the central element in Janey's Childhood. Excelling in art throughout her school years Janey devoted herself to the art course provided by Balcatta Senior High school, where her passion for art only intensified.

Janey has been painting full-time since 1991 and has attained a high degree of respect in the art world from peers and art lovers alike. Janey has won numerous distinguished artistic awards for her work and has sold many paintings throughout Australia and overseas. Janey Emery is achieving the recognition her distinctive artistic talents deserve.

Janey is Self-Taught in All Mediums with the exception of leisure courses undertaken in oil and water colours.

Art has always played a part of who I am. From early childhood to now there has been a need for me to express myself through drawing and painting. I find peace in my craft, and I hope I bring that to my paintings.

To me, my Art is like breathing. Painting is my life.

Janey Emery

https://www.janeyemery.art/

Chronology

Another note from the author, Stephan De Jonghe

My "from astronomy to mythology" series of novellas posed some difficulties in terms of writing the stories into a logical chronology. Until the Iliad, and the Odessey, no one had ever written any of the tales of titan's forming the world, or their ultimate defeat by the gods who eventually resided in Mount Olympus. These stories were imagined piecemeal, embellished, refined, and retold over a thousand-year period. Unlike history, which did happen on a linear timeline and can be plotted, the timeline used in fictional stories were not relevant, and by their very nature at the whim of the story teller. Over the millennia, re-tellers of the stories frequently added details, and characters that were often inconsistent with the other stories. No one knew and no one cared, as they were mostly just for entertainment.

For the more serious devotees, these stories were the basis for a religion, and many aspects of the stories were used to focus worshippers' attention, and they were therefore treated by many at the time as historical facts. They focused their attention on those gods and goddesses that were consistent with their beliefs and values.

The best example that I can use to demonstrate the challenge of chronology, is referencing a main character known as Pandora. As she is the first human woman, she features in her own story, but she was created by Hephaestus, the son of Zeus and Hera, and it happened when Zeus and Hera were already married. But Zeus met and fell in love with Europa, a human woman, who was alive before he married Hera, and before he had a son to ask to make the first woman. Challenging!

As an author with a particular attention to detail, (at least I believe I do), the chronology of Greek mythological events became increasing important to me as the list of novellas planned for this series grew to thirteen.

I have therefore prepared a simple chronology (that may or may not be consistent with other writers of this genre) to assist readers in sorting out the sequence of events that occur in the stories that I am sharing with you. (Spoiler alert!)

I now believe that Greek Mythology Chronology should be a legitimised field of study all on its own. (Perhaps it already is?)

The novella.	The details of the event.
Pisces	Gaia forms the earth, oceans and skies. She is the earth mother.
Pisces	Gaia gives birth to Uranus.
Pisces	Cronus is born and defeats Uranus when he is released from confinement.
Pisces	Aphrodite is born.
Capricorn	Pricus is the father of the sea-goats.
Pisces	Cronus is crowned king and marries Rea. Zeus is one of their six children.
Centaurus	Cronus mates with Philyra. Chiron is born.
Pandora	Prometheus creates a race of human men - It is known as the golden age.
Pisces	Zeus defeats Cronus and Zeus is crowned King of the Gods.

Pisces	Zeus marries Metis, Athena is born, but Metis dies.
Pandora	Prometheus creates a second race of human men - It is known as the silver age.
Pandora	Prometheus creates a third race of human men - It is known as the bronze age.
Pisces	Zeus marries but then quickly divorces Themis.
Pandora	Prometheus creates a fourth race of human men - It is known as the iron age.
Sagittarius	Crotus invents the bow and arrow.
Pisces	Zeus marries Hera. Ares, Eileithyia, Hephaestus, and Hebe are born.
Pisces	Aphrodite arrives at Mount Olympus and marries Hephaestus.
Pandora	Hephaestus creates Pandora as the first human woman.
Taurus	Zeus meets Europa.
Scorpio	Zeus mates with Leto and Apollo and Artemis are born.
Scorpio	Poseidon mates with Euryale and Orion is born.
Scorpio	Atalanta is recused as an infant and she now runs with Artemis
Aries	Zeus creates a cloud nymph named Nephele.
Aries	Poseidon mates with Theophane and Chrysomallos is born.
Aries	Nephele marries Athamas and Helle and Phrixus are born.
Aries	Chrysomallos rescues Helle and Phrixus.
Ophiuchus	Apollo mates with Coronis and Asclepius is born.
Cancer/Leo	Zeus mates with Alkmene and Herakles is born.

Gemini	Zeus mates with Leda and Polydeuces and Castor are born.
Pisces	Aphrodite mates with Ares. Eros is born.
Scorpio	Orion meets and befriends Hephaistos.
Virgo/Libra	Zeus visits Themis and Astraea.
Cancer/Leo	Herakles is assigned the first of his ten labours.
Cancer/Leo	Herakles befriends Chiron.
Centaurus	Chiron befriends Herakles.
Gemini	Castor and Polydeuces join the Argo crew
Cancer/Leo	Herakles joins Argo crew.
Gemini	Atalanta asks to join Argo crew.
Scorpio	Orion meets Artemis.
Centaurus	Chiron commences as a teacher.
Gemini	Herakles is inadvertently separated from the Argo.
Cancer/Leo	Herakles resumes his labours.
Scorpio	Orion duels with the giant scorpion.
Gemini	Jason and Argo crew return with the Golden Fleece.
Gemini	Calydonian Boar Hunt.
Gemini	Atalanta joins the Calydonian Boar Hunt
Cancer/Leo	Herakles accidentally wounds Chiron
Centaurus	Chiron makes his plea to Zeus.
Pisces	The Greeks and the Trojans start a war that lasts ten years.
Aquarius	Zeus meets Ganymede.
Cancer/Leo	Herakles becomes immortal and marries Hebe.
Pisces	Atalanta competes in a running race against her potential suitors.
Gemini	Castor and Polydeuces become immortal.
Pisces	Aphrodite an Eros escape Typhon.

Authors note

Authors note: This story is based on Greek mythology. The name Pandora means "the one who bears all gifts." This story posed many challenges as its timeline within the mythology doesn't fit well with the other stories. It can't be helped, so please accept writers' license for this anomaly.

Many of these stories owe some of their earlier history to the Phoenicians, Babylonians, and Mycenaean's, and were initially used to help ancient travelers remember star patterns as a nighttime navigational tool. Over time, these fascinating stories were greatly embellished on how the constellations came to be formed. The ancient Greeks called these constellations the "Katasterismoi" meaning, "the placing of the stars." They gave names and told stories about forty-eight out of the eighty-eight constellations that are recognised by the International Astronomical Union.

These mythologies were embellished as they were countlessly re-told with tales of gods encountering wild creatures, fighting fierce battles, and of course having lots of sex. After all, these men were away from home for lengthy periods of time. They shared these stories to entertain urban dwellers that they encountered, and from there the stories became legends, and for many people they became their religion.

A Greek poet and storyteller named Homer, was the first person to document these stories and he is most famous for the "Iliad" and the "Odyssey" which he composed some 2,800 years ago. Whilst very little is known about Homer, he is regarded by many as the founder of modern literature. His two main works were the first literary works to be taught formally to students.

Interestingly, there are thirty-three film adaptations of the Odyssey, proving his works are still relevant to modern audiences.

Later, a poet named Hesiod, significantly contributed to Greek mythology and followed on from Homer's work. Together they are attributed with establishing ancient Greek religious customs, formal astronomy, the development of structured learning, documenting events, early economics, commercial farming, and time keeping.

The word "zodiac" originated from the Greek words "Zodiakos kuklos," meaning "circle of little animals". It wasn't until 50BCE that the first classical zodiac depicting the twelve astrological star signs in their current order was first depicted. It is known as the "Dendera zodiac."

During the 2nd century CE, a Greco-Roman astrologer and astronomer named Claudius Ptolemy worked on his documented Tetrabiblos into what is regarded as western astrology's primary source document and remains largely in use today. Also of note is that astronomers have named a crater on the Luna surface, and another on the surface of the planet Mars Ptolemaeus, in honour of Ptolemy and his contribution to astronomy. The connection between Greek names and Roman names for the same deities came from their translation from one language to the other. In ancient Greek, Zeus is pronounced Dias. In Latin that became Djous Pater (Sky father) or Luppiter. In English this became Jupiter. Many names evolved in this way.

As an author, my goal is to turn what is known of the mythology, into an enjoyable story for today's reader.

Stephan J De Jonghe

The Story of Pandora

Gaia was the first. A Titan, Gaia was our earth mother, and from her came her children who ruled over all her creation. Her first born was Uranus, a male Titan baby that she created in her own womb. He loved his mother and when he came of age, she made him lord of the skies so that he could surround her with his love. Between them, they conceived many children, but Uranus secretly confined all of them into the deep bowels of the earth, as he could not tolerate sharing his mother's affections. Finally, Cronus, the youngest Titan sibling managed to alert Gaia to their plight. Gaia was furious and the earth rumbled and groaned and she vented her son from deep below the surface and so he was freed.

Reunited with his mother, Cronus and Gaia plotted to punish Uranus. They successfully executed their plan and Uranus was humbled into submission. They next released Cronus' brothers and sisters. After their victory and in celebration, Gaia granted them all dominion of the oceans, seas, rivers, mountains, forests, and grass plains. They became the Titans who ruled the earth, the sun, and the moon, and everyone, except for Uranus, felt safe and happy.

Cronus was crowned King of all the Titan's by his siblings as he was their hero, saviour, and he was also the strongest. For a really long time the Titans were guardians of all aspects of the earth, winds, waters, and life on earth.

One day, Cronus began to feel that the Titans were all becoming weak and lazy. The Earth was theirs, the rivers flowed, the forests grew, animals roamed, storms billowed, and truly there wasn't much for anyone to do. So, he consulted Prometheus, son of Lapetus, and favoured nephew. Cronus knew his nephew was creative, wise, and thoughtful. He had knowledge of things to come and could predict future events with amazing accuracy and reliability. He was a forward thinker. Of Lapetus four sons it was Prometheus who would best understand, and so it would be he that would devise a solution to their increasingly apparent problems.

'A lethargy has struck the Titans, Prometheus,' Cronus said, explaining his concern to the younger Titan.

'I have sensed this also, Uncle,' Prometheus nodded agreeing with the king. 'I have given it some thought.'

Cronus smiled at him. Prometheus never agreed with him just because he knew it was proper that he should. He only agreed with what he also believed was right. Whilst he never argued, he always spoke his mind, and Cronus respected him for that. The others bowed readily, almost scraping their foreheads on the floor before him whenever he challenged them. They were practically useless in discussions about difficult tasks, or serious problems. Prometheus was the exception.

'What do you suggest we do?' asked Cronus. They were seated in comfortable chairs overlooking the ocean which was calm. The sun warmed them. They sipped from goblets enjoying nectar and they grazed from a food platter filled with tasty cured meats, cheeses, fruits, eggs, nuts, and bread rolls, that Rhea, Cronus' wife, had prepared for them.

Prometheus drew in a deep breath before he answered. 'As Titans we draw our energy from engaging in tasks. The busier we are, the more energy we have. When we have problems to solve, we become more productive. I believe we need more responsibilities. My Grandmother has given us this bounty, and we all share in its guardianship, but now we need to do more than simply maintain it. If we don't, we'll all become fat, lazy, and stupid.'

'You have been thinking this through,' Cronus concluded. He absentmindedly rubbed the ever-increasing size of his paunch.

'We have created the forests and fields and we have populated them with a wide variety of animals. The balance between them is perfect and so we have little to do to manage their numbers,' Prometheus continued.

Cronus just nodded. He had roamed the forests and the fields. He and his brothers had hunted, and others had gathered fruits and vegetables that were plentiful. Their small harvest of the rich food supply could never adversely affect the balance of life that they managed and supported.

'We need to create a race of beings, in our own image, and we should grant them the ability to speak and to learn. More importantly we need to teach them to respect and worship us as their Gods,' Prometheus explained, but then he stopped to gauge his uncle's reaction.

'Continue.'

'I suggest we start with a small herd. In that way we can observe their antics and learn from them. We'll scrutinize their behaviours and modify our management of them based on our observations.'

'How do we begin?' Cronus enthused, clearly supporting his nephew's plan. He leaned forward and Prometheus recognised the motion as acceptance and agreement with what he was suggesting. He was happy, as his uncle was hard to predict, and often harder to please.

'As with all the animals, I will mould them from the clay and the soil. They will be in our image. They won't have any godly powers, but they'll all eat and drink as we do. They will walk and run as we do. They will also talk, sing, and laugh,' Prometheus smiled as he prepared himself to reveal the most important role these creatures will have. 'And... we will teach them to revere us.'

Cronus smiled. The boy had brains. He had the answers. He could do this, and it would create an interest for all Titans, and this would energize them. Titans needed to be worshipped, but worshipping each other grew tiresome. These creatures would be taught to do so willingly, and eagerly, and that'll be good for all Titans. 'Prometheus, what shall we call these creatures?'

'Collectively, we'll call them Men. Individually, they will be known as a Man. I'll use the rich humus from local soil, clay, and dirt, and mould them into creation.'

'Why humus?' Cronus queried.

'Humus can hold ninety percent of its weight in water.' Prometheus explained. 'They'll need this high level of fluid to distribute fluids and nutrients and to eliminate wastes.'

'Humus men.' Coronus pondered the idea. Then he smiled and decreed, 'Hu-men.'

***

Prometheus immediately got busy moulding the first ever group of male humans from local clay and soil. He named the first man he created, Pelasgus, knowing that he'd be one-day known historically as the ancient one, in honour of his being the first ever man. He next thought up good names for the other men he formed as he brought them to life. He was responsible and did not name any of them after the Titans. He fashioned the other humans from Pelasgus' form, giving them all slight variations in height, weight, and in particular, their facial features. He decided that they should all be males as he felt that females would negatively affect behaviour, and they would distort the lessons learnt from their creation. He also decided that they should live a life of plenty with abundant food, water, and comfort.

The men were taught to be obedient to the gods which they did willingly and happily. They were occupied with labouring and attending to the trees that bore fruit and the fields that grew wild vegetables, that they gathered as food for both the Titans and themselves. A stream was created to supply them with clean drinking water. The stream flowed into a lake and this gave them a place to bathe, swim, and frolic. The climate was perfect for them, never being too hot or too cold. Gentle rains came at night to refresh the outdoors, and soft breezes kept the air sweet and clean. They lived in groups in comfortable caves with soft bedding. Wild beasts were kept away with barriers and so they were no threat to the humans. The men had few skills, no weapons, or any other means to protect themselves as they were kept safe by the Titans.

Everyone was always happy. The men lived their lives free from pain, cares, sorrows, fears, or anxieties. They had no sickness and did not suffer from the aches and pains of aging. The men never argued, fought, or waged war. They had no claim on possessions, or had any need to have things that they weren't readily willing to share. They laughed often, shared stories, played music, sang, and danced.

They were never aroused, had no need for intimacy or sexual release, or any interest in permanent relationships. These men could not have children and they didn't even know what a child was. They had all arrived to this place without questioning, and they never became curious about their creation.

These men had no need for laws, police, or judges, as they only knew fairness, cooperation and kindness. The men never travelled to other places as they had just known that they had everything they needed at home. They were obedient to the Titan's and they contentedly lived their lives. It was a golden age for the humans.

Then, one day, they all just died.

It seemed that they all died peacefully in their sleep. Whilst the Titan's never discovered the true cause of their human's demise, they did conclude that their life was too easy. They had no important purpose, and therefore no reason to live. They determined that they needed to modify human activity, and behaviour, for when they tried creating a race of humans for the second time.

***

The second creation of humanity was delayed by the Titanomachy. Zeus, youngest son of Cronus, avoided his sibling's fate and later freed them from their father's stomach. They united in battle against the Titan's and the ensuring war lasted for a very long time. The Titan's fought off numerous assaults from the next generation who were known as God's, but under Zeus' command, the Gods and Goddesses prevailed. As a result, most of the Titans were banished.

Not all of the Titans sided with Cronus. Prometheus could foresee Zeus' victory and eventual elevation to King of all of the God's. So, he and his brother Epimetheus chose to fight with Zeus and so were spared banishment at the end of the war. The two joined the Gods at their new home at Mount Olympus. Zeus however, remained cautious of Prometheus' and Epimetheus' due to their lineage.

***

When Zeus became settled as the King, he summoned Prometheus to discuss the next human experiment. He had heard stories of how the first batch had failed, and he believed that they should try again. Prometheus happily detailed what they had done and the reasoning he used to explain why the creation of mankind had failed.

'I had believed that if we provided them with all their needs, such as food, water, companionship, and shelter, that they would thrive. They seemed happy enough, they were never sick or injured, so when they died it was both a sad moment, and a mystifying one.' Prometheus had been careful not to describe Cronus' involvement, or refer to any of the other now banished Titan's that had participated in the first experimental creation of humans. It was better to focus on what they should do better the next time they tried it.

'Did these humans worship their gods?' Zeus queried.

'In a fashion,' Prometheus replied. 'They were told that they were required to worship, but I'm now convinced that they had no compelling reason to do so,' Prometheus concluded. He then added, 'The men had a good life, but they were bored. Even I became bored watching them, and whilst I was sad at their deaths, I was also excited about the prospect of trying the experiment again, but with significant modifications.'

'To your design, or to their purpose?' Zeus was curious.

'My design is fine, but they do need more variances in their environment. They need to be forced into learning how to provide and fend for themselves. They need to feel fear in order to feel alive. They need to experience yearning, so that they can learn gratitude. The first group could not respect, or truly appreciate their bounty, as they didn't have to do anything to earn it.' Prometheus paused. 'Zeus, we need humans and I'd like to try it again.'

'I agree that we need humans. We need them to fear us, and to worship us. Managing them will give us purpose. Their belief in us, and more importantly their fear of us, will give us our strength. I worry that without human worshippers we will fade away, much the same way the first batch of humans perished.' Zeus paused as he reflected on the importance of what he had just said. Verbalizing it, had made it clearer in his own mind. He smiled and continued, 'I want you to create a second group of men,' he ordered.

Prometheus accepted the command enthusiastically.

So, Prometheus changed things for the second group of men. He still fashioned them from clay and soil. Their forms were the same as before, but their minds were very different. The gods formed seasons for these new men and they were subjected to hot summers and cold winters, so they had to leave the caves and rough shelters and construct solid housing. The fruits from the forest were no longer abundant, and so they had to cultivate the land and plant crops. These men were simple and immature. They were quick to anger, rage, and jealousy. They became increasingly greedy in their quest to own better things, and many of them wanted power to control the will of the others. They formed cliques and relationships. They suffered from want and desire. They committed random and reckless acts of violence against each other, and there were many injuries and some deaths. They also failed to honour the gods properly, so Zeus destroyed them by casting them to be spirits in the underworld.

After a brief period, this silver age of men, was over.

***

It took a long time before Prometheus could bring himself to discuss his second failure in creating a race of humans with Zeus. He felt he understood what had gone wrong this time, and he was on the verge of modifying humans' teachings, when Zeus had abruptly ended his experiment. But he also knew that the God's needed human worshipers, and that he'd be given another chance.

When Zeus summoned Prometheus, he outlaid his plan. 'This time I want you to fashion the humans from Ash trees. It is possible that the clay and earth soiled their brains and that they were too stupid to understand their purpose.'

Prometheus nodded his agreement. Ash trees would work, it would take longer, but perhaps Zeus was onto something, as Ash was more durable than clay and soil.

When the third group of human males were ready, Zeus himself personally issued instructions to the assembled men. 'Your purpose is to learn to fight. You'll learn to construct weapons from the metals that you will mine from the soil. You'll develop skills with these weapons, and you'll practice them with each other. You will use them to hunt the bear, boar, lions, and other wild beasts, but you'll work together as a team, and you'll never use your weapons in anger against each other.'

The assembled men smiled and looked about each other. The thought of weapons, hunting, and fighting, greatly appealed to them.

'In return for your existence, I order you to erect shrines and statues in our honour. Kill in our honour and die knowing your God's love you.'

The men seemed pensive so Zeus, understanding his own lust and passions, added another feature to their lives. 'I will also grant you the power of arousal. You will enjoy intimacy with each other.'

So, the men mined bronze and fashioned weapons. They built sturdier houses and decorated them with weapons and the spoils of the hunt. They formed relationships and were sexually intimate. The most common form of metal they mined and forged was bronze, and so they became known among the gods as the bronze age of mankind.

Over time, the stronger men enslaved the weaker men and used them as sex slaves. Under threat of banishment, or beatings, they forced them to grow crops, fetch water, and do all the cooking and cleaning. The stronger warriors eventually turned on each other, fighting viciously for dominance, and many of them died in painful agony. They were so busy fighting, and fornicating, that they forgot to honour the God's, so Zeus cast these men into Hades also.

***

Zeus avoided meeting with Prometheus for a long time. His latest plan for the humans had failed terribly. He had truly believed that violence, and their fear of death, would bring about man's strong and unconditional faith in the Gods and that they'd worship them for their powers. Fear was always a significant motivator, as was personal greed for power. Zeus admitted to himself that his warrior race of men was a failure, and that he did not know what to do next. They clearly needed to have worshippers and followers for the energy they exuded, and the tasks they could perform in the service of their God's.

When Prometheus was finally able to consult with Zeus, he had already formulated a plan of how to repeat the launch of humanity with numerous refinements to all the previous attempts.

'I think we create them and then just leave them alone to develop naturally,' Prometheus explained. 'Some may die, but those that survive will quickly learn what it means to work, share, cooperate, and hopefully, they'll thrive. I think we need to let them work out for themselves their reverence for us as God's. When they take ownership of the process it will become deeply ingrained into their minds and culture. We were wrong to think that we could order obedience and reverence to us. They must give it willingly, or it has no value.'

'Do it,' Zeus agreed, but his features remained impassive.

'I would also like to add human females into the human population...'

'What!' Zeus roared ad his face reddened. Do you realise what the risk that would be? I know from personal experience that all males behave stupidly for the sake of a female's affection. I think it is far too soon to talk about introducing women. Work out the problems with the men first, and I'll consider allowing the creation of women later.'

And so, for the fourth time, a new breed of men was created up from the ground. They became the men born of the Iron Age. They were simple, base men, and they would readily cheat, and scheme, to fulfill their greed. Their lives were filled with the need to constantly work and they hunted to feed, clothe, and shelter themselves. They mined precious metals and stones and then gave them value. With increased wealth, the wealthy found they had power and control over the poor. They eventually developed the concept of ownership over the land, marked out boundaries, and denied access to others to partake in the bounty of the lands that they controlled. They used innovative weapons to forcibly take ownership of the other men's possessions. They used equal violence to defend their property, fully believing there claim of ownership. For a long time, chaos ensued and the men were unhappy and lived in fear of everything.

Slowly, as Prometheus predicted, the power struggles subsided and permanent leaders were agreed upon. Many men willingly became subservient to other stronger men for survival. Some formed relationship with others and were intimate and caring. As couples and as groups, they grew crops, raised farm animals, built homes and villages, and they especially learned how to revere the Gods and be grateful for all material possessions, their health, and their lives. Increasingly, the men asked the gods to be granted females so that they have wives to breed with to increase their numbers, as they have seen domestic animals do.

***

It was about this time that a committee of men approached Prometheus to create for them the perfect beast to raise on their farms. The result was the creation of the cow and the bull. These cattle were perfect for meat, milk, clothing, and footwear.

Prometheus next attempted to deceive Zeus in the division of the choice cuts of the meat. Humans ended up having the prime cuts, and the Gods were left with the bones and the offal. Due to their rivalry, Prometheus was denied permission for the men to cook the meat. They were ordered into eating it raw.

Zeus was still so outraged, that he decided he would additionally punish Prometheus by assigning the task of designing the first woman to his son, Hephaestus. In this way human females could be designed to Zeus' specifications and not to Prometheus'. Zeus knew that Prometheus plans for women were that they'd be compliant and demure. Zeus wanted human women to have spirit and character, so that they'd torment human males in the same way the goddesses tormented the male gods. Also, Zeus was now bored with sex, and he hoped that the introduction of some feisty human females would offer new excitements. Prometheus was devastated with the announcement.

Prometheus felt desperate. He felt that the woman that Zeus commissioned would become a curse on human males. He desperately wanted to intercede. He wanted to be responsible for her learning, and training, before she was introduced into the human male population. If he couldn't design her body, then perhaps, he could shape her mind. He met with Zeus and asked for permission to marry the first woman human.

Zeus laughed and said it was a preposterous idea and so denied it. Prometheus was crestfallen. His dream of completing the human race was robbed from him.

***

Zeus would meet with Hephaestus and tell him that he had decided that the honour of being tasked to create the first female human would be bestowed on him. As father and son, they were sometimes the best of friends, but often the worst of enemies. Hephaestus, or Heph as many called him, was the God of blacksmiths, metal workers, carpenters, craftsmen, artisans, sculptors, inventors, and metallurgists. He had power over fire and ruled the volcanoes. Heph was a master craftsman and responsible for the invention and construction of many things. He was also a go to person that often Zeus relied upon.

His permanent limp was brought on by an earlier physical confrontation with his father. The resultant blow permanently damaged both his body and his confidence. Sadly, Heph struggled with forming intimate relationships with females. His skill sets with women were much tested when he became in love with Aphrodite.

The meeting that Zeus had with his son Hephaestus was brief. Zeus was seated on a comfortable chair before an ornate meals table in the living quarters of Heph's workshop. Before them were two goblets of wine, which they both sipped from without enthusiasm. Zeus studied his son intensely. Heph was simultaneously a nuisance but also highly beneficial to his father. Zeus both respected and despised him, and his feelings for this son alternated between needing him, and wishing that he'd permanently depart Mount Olympus. Presently, he needed him.

'I want you to create a human woman,' Zeus explained to Heph.

Heph stared blankly at his father. Zeus' well-known habit of lengthy pauses between uttering the details of the requests and demands made of him were annoying. He knew from experience that it was better to wait patiently to hear more of the details, before responding. His father had an annoying habit of changing tact if he thought you could anticipate what he was going to say or ask for.

'I want her to be beautiful, alluring, graceful, confident, and most of all, feisty. She will become the first woman and therefore, if successful, she'd become the mould for many more human females,' Zeus elaborated.

Heph nodded.

Zeus smiled. He did not need to ask Heph if he could accomplish this feat, because he already knew that he could. He didn't need to ask if he'd do this task, because he knew he would. He didn't need to ask how long it would take, because he already knew that it would take as long as was needed. He didn't concern himself with the quality of the craftsmanship, because he already knew she'd be perfect. He considered asking what materials his son would use, but refrained from doing so, because he realised that he neither cared, nor wanted to hear Heph's protracted, and overly detailed response. Heph often over-elaborated.

'Thank you for the wine,' Zeus said and drained his goblet as he arose from the chair, placing the empty before Heph. Without another word, he walked down the stairs and exited the building.

***

Hephaestus decided he'd carve the woman from clay. The first stage of constructing such a large-scale statue of a woman required a strong wire frame. Heph needed to work on her in a standing position so that he could properly carve her contours. He first assembled the frame for the head and torso. Next, he assembled the two arms and hands, and lastly the legs and feet. He attached the five sections together, mounted her on a platform, and stood back to examine his progress. He was pleased, and could see the basic image of the future woman standing before him.

Heph had an abundant source of quality working clay from the river Alfeios, that flowed nearby to Mount Olympus. His workers mined the moist clay and transported it to his workshop so he always had a ready supply. The grey clay was made from ground quartz, mica, iron, and was perfect to work with. He added water to make the clay slippery and workable. His hands worked deftly and he often dunked them into the water bucket to maintain the pliability of the material. As he worked, he poured in the sodium silicate that he had developed for this purpose. This discovery set him apart from other clay sculptors, and it was his closely guarded secret, as it maintained the even consistency of the material.

After crafting her basic shape, he started adding the finer details. Starting with her face, he realised that he was becoming physically attracted to the woman forming before him. This enthused him further, and he continued working long into the night, having floodlit the area with fires bouncing their light off the reflective screens he had set up around his work station. This gave him an even and steady source of light with which to work. His workers maintained the fires and brought him food and refreshments. They were experienced enough to understand their master's obsessive compulsion to keep working.

As the clay hardened, he was able to add expression to her form, He added her eyes, ears, nose and was particularly careful with her lips. Her chin was noble. Her brow made her seem wise and proud. He next refocused on her eyes as he wanted to make them smile. He wanted her to be both appealing and alluring. He had made her legs long and shapely and added her perfect feet and slender toes. Her arms were long and slender. Her hands and fingers were graceful and delicate. He was tempted to give her over-sized breasts, but decided that they should be perfectly proportioned, and in keeping with her slender waistline. He hesitated fashioning her genitalia as he had little experience. He decided that he'd consult with Athena about this area of her body. Athena was also Zeus' daughter and a highly respected goddess. She was a conservative, knowledgeable, generous to her friends, and was a close friend to Heph.

Athena was always welcome and readily available when invited to visit him in his workshop. She was happy to assist him, readily agreeing with him about the importance of getting these details correct. She was practical about such matters, and instructed him on the finer details of the intimate parts of the female form.

***

Later, as the clay started to harden, Hephaestus realised that he had modelled the first human woman after Athena. He was tempted to leave her as he'd created her, but then thought of the consequences. Firstly, Zeus wouldn't like it as was his daughter, and even Zeus had boundaries. Secondly, Athena wouldn't want any credit for her, or want to be thought off in this way, as she espoused herself as being the modest goddess. Lastly, Hephaestus concluded that any human woman that he carved in Athena's image might be seen by others as an act of loneliness on his part, and he didn't want anyone's pity. He made some modifications to her cheek bones and chin, altering her profile away from looking like the goddess of wisdom, war, and oddly enough, handcraft.

As they clay hardened, he used a firm paper embedded with fine grains of sand grit to smooth off any remaining rough edges. He then set her aside and started to clean the room as she dried.

***

Over the next seven days, the clay model of the first human woman dried on the modelling platform. While she dried, Hephaestus set to work blending the colours for the glazing. Making her the perfect shape was only phase one of this enormous task. He now had to paint her so that her skin tones were vivid and lively. He made several batches of slightly different shades so that he could merge them evenly onto her surface, depending on where he was applying the glaze. When satisfied with the pigments of the glaze, he set about to prepare her hair. He had collected the off cuts from several accommodating goddesses, and he slowly, painstakingly, added each strand into her scalp. Her skin tone would be a slightly darker hue, and so different to Athena's paler skin tones. He hoped that the distinction would remove any remaining resemblance to his half-sisters' features.

When he was satisfied that the sculpture was completely dry, and free from dust, he commenced applying the under glaze, and letting it dry before applying the layers of colour glaze. He decided on four coats in total, allowing each to properly dry before applying the next. When he was satisfied with the final result, and she was completely dry, he applied the final transparent coat to lock in his artwork. He left her to dry once more and he ordered his men to fire up the kiln.

This kiln was supersized by his normal standards. Hephaestus had been commissioned to make many clay products, and so he had numerous kilns of varying sizes to suit the size of the firing. The clay sculpture fitted into the kiln neatly. He checked that the fire was at the correct temperature and the firing commenced as soon as he manoeuvred her into the stone cabinet.

Due to the size of the statue, the baking process took over a day to complete. He and his workers rostered themselves to keep the heat at a constant temperature, and Hephaestus himself was able to catch up on some well-earned sleep as the first ever human woman was baked off, much like a bun in the oven.

***

The following day, he allowed the fires to die down, and the woman to cool sufficiently so she could be safely removed from the oven. He waited until she was able to be touched by the back of his hand without feeling any heat before he moved her. Gently, he and his team guided her from the kiln and into the room.

They all stared at her perfection. Some of the men gasped, her form clearly exceeding expectations. His men were all sworn to secrecy about the work that they did for Hephaestus, but he could tell that on this occasion, that they would fail dismally. He realised that word of her creation would spread quickly throughout the male population and that it would create some excitement.

After examining her for hairline cracks and finding none, Heph asked his leading hand to invite Athena back into the workshop. He needed someone who he trusted, to be the first to examine his handy work, before inviting Zeus to inspect the result.

It didn't take her long to arrive. Athena was prepared with clothing that she had specially made for the newly crafted woman. She also gasped at her beauty, and hugged Heph in congratulations for his craftsmanship, and dedication. She would become the perfect woman to complement mankind.

'She can't remain naked,' Athena remonstrated Heph playfully. 'A woman should be attired in clothing befitting her station.'

Athena removed a magnificent silvery gown from the bag she had carried with her. It had silk veils which she herself had embroidered for the woman to be dressed in, when she was granted life. She held it up for Heph to see and was delighted when he showed that he was impressed with her work.

'We won't be able to dress her in that, until she is limber,' Heph explained. For now, he covered her form with a dark, red-rose coloured cloak, that he had prepared for that purpose.

'We're now ready to invite Zeus to examine her, and hopefully, approve of her.' Heph explained.

***

It didn't take long for Zeus to arrive after being informed that the first human woman was ready for his inspection. Clearly, this project was significant to Zeus and when he arrived, he was grinning like an excited teenage boy who was about to meet his fantasy woman.

'Show me, show me, show me,' he commanded.

Hephaestus withdrew the cloak revealing his clay statue to his father.

Zeus involuntarily gasped. He slowly paced the room in a circle around her. 'How do we...'

'Animate her?' Heph finished the question for his father.

'Yes.'

'If you approve, we will need to breathe life into her.'

'Of course. Summon the winds, all of them.' Zeus commanded softly. He couldn't shift his gaze away from the female statue.

Suddenly, the air moved and swirled about them. Documents and plans wafted on Heph's work bench. Soon the four winds materialised into their human form. They stood in a circle around the statue of the woman, but said nothing.

Boreas was the God of the north wind, the cold, storms, and the bringer of winter. He was powerful and prone to temper. His passion was horses and he loved to ride with them as swift as the wind. He would one day be credited with saving Athens from destruction by the Persian army and navy. His storm would sink their fleet of four hundred ships, each brimming with Persian warriors.

Notos was the south wind, associated with high temperatures and was the bringer of summer. When enraged he could also destroy crops by desiccating them.

Eurus was the east wind. When he was upset, he could become turbulent and was often criticised by mariners. He was often in the company of Helios, God of the sun, and they often arrived together during the dawn.

Zephyrus was the west wind. He was the gentlest of all the wind gods and brought spring to the people. He was involved with the trees bearing fruits, and therefore the most popular of all the wind gods.

'Which of you will breathe life into this woman?' Zeus asked them when the dust had settled.

'I will,' Zephyrus replied. The three other wind gods nodded in agreement and consent. Zephyrus was the most benevolent of them, and he had the aptitude to be both graceful and respectful. He swirled into action, surrounding the statue and focused on her nose and mouth, entering her and filling her with life giving air. Immediately her chest heaved, her breasts lifting as she drew in lungsful of cool fresh air. Her heart commenced beating and her complexion reddened. She fell to the floor and was immediately scooped up by Heph and he rested her gently on his bed. Athena then draped the sheet over her, covering her body, leaving only her head exposed.

'Why did she fall?' Zeus was concerned.

'Her muscles will need time to develop and become strong enough to support her weight,' Heph explained.

Zeus nodded his thanks to Zephyrus who had re-materialized as soon as she was breathing.

'She hasn't opened her eyes. Is she okay?' Zeus asked anxiously.

'She has only just been granted life,' Athena admonished. 'You'll need to give her some time to adjust.

Zeus turned to Heph. 'You have done excellent work, my son. Although, I shouldn't be surprised given your skills and reputation, but I'm delighted with her, I really am. She looks amazing. What happens next to her?'

'Firstly,' Heph looked at Athena for support. She nodded. 'We need to teach her the basics of movement. After she opens her eyes, all sights and sounds will need to be introduced to her. Doing this properly now will show us how to do this process quickly when we want to increase the number of women we create.'

'Steady on,' Zeus cautioned. 'Shouldn't we test out this one before we plan a whole herd of them?'

Heph smiled. He would have preferred the term, tribe, but he knew what his father meant.

'Next, we'll teach her to comprehend language, and how to talk,' Heph continued.

Zeus was tempted to refrain her from being a speaking woman, but capitulated to the logic of it. He eventually nodded his approval.

'We need to teach her values,' Athena spoke adding to the dialogue. 'We need to bestow her all the gifts of virtue, so that she is the perfect role model for all other human women.'

'That will be a difficult task,' Zeus conceded. 'We certainly have enough experience to avoid teaching her the worst values. 'Involve all the gods and goddesses. Make her training a group task. All of us will benefit from her, so all of us should be involved in her teaching and training.'

***

Shortly after Zeus and the four winds departed, the woman opened her eyes. She saw Heph and Athena studying her, looking all concerned and so she instinctively frowned at them.

'How do you feel?' Athena asked.

The woman looked blankly at Athena. She hadn't heard these sounds before and failed to understand the meaning of the question.

Athena sat beside her and stroked the woman's arm. She fell asleep and slept for many days.

Sometime later, Zeus sent Hermès to visit with them to learn about the woman's progress. Hermès was also a son of Zeus, and was the messenger of the gods. He was often sent on errands, such as this, by his father. Hermès was one of the few gods who could freely travel to the underworld and return. In this capacity he often guided the dead to his uncle, Hades.

The woman was now awake and looked curiously at Hermès. He was someone new.

'She's fascinating,' Hermès decreed, smiling at her whilst staring. 'What is her name?'

'We haven't given her one yet?' Heph conceded.

'May I?' Hermès begged.

Heph looked at Athena and she shrugged. 'Sure. Why not. She needs a name and we'd appreciate hearing your suggestion,' Heph invited.

Hermès looked closely at the woman and examined her. 'She's truly a magnificent gift to both the gods and humanity and so I'll name her, "Pandora."'

The woman looked blankly at Hermès, and he was sad that his suggestion hadn't solicited a happy response from her.

'She can't hear or speak,' Athena explained.

'We haven't got that far yet,' Heph added.

Hermès looked at Heph and Athena. He next looked at the woman and moved a chair to sit nearer to her. He placed his hands on her throat. She wasn't afraid, or even worried, as she had no concept of fear or concern for her life. The others watched Hermès as he gently caressed her neck and mouth. Later, he delicately massaged her ears and then softly tugged on her nose. Lastly, he placed one hand on her forehead and held it in place.

They were fascinated watching Hermès as he worked his godly powers giving her the power of hearing, smell, taste, and control over her voice.

He finished and stood up. 'Hello,' he said smiling at her. 'Can you hear me, Pandora?'

She smiled and nodded.

'Can you speak to us?' Athena asked.

'I think so,' came her croaky garbled reply.

'Your name is Pandora. Can you say your name, Pandora?'

'Pandora,' she repeated and smiled. She nodded excitedly and clearly enjoyed the sound of her name. Heph, Hermès, and Athena all laughed, delighted by her happiness.

'Well done,' Heph praised.

And so, over many days and nights, the three of them taught the woman how to understand words, to speak, and eventually even how to think. She learned to eat and quickly formed vocalised opinions about what foods she preferred. They taught her how to sit up, stand, and momentarily she was walking. She was now dressed in the silver gown that Athena had crafted for her, but she wore with it with some complaint, saying that she'd preferred to be naked. All of them laughed and insisted that learning to wear clothing was a vital part of her training.

One day after they had eaten, Heph went to his work station and picked up an ornate beautiful golden crown and placed it on her head. 'I crown you, Pandora. First of many women.'

Athena picked up a shiny surface and placed it before Pandora, showing her for the first time her own reflection. Pandora wept happily and smiled and they were all overjoyed for her.

Hermès next returned to his father to detail Pandora's progress. He explained about her ability to move about, speak, and comprehend. 'She's magnificent,' he concluded.

'That good.'

'She'll need a husband to guide her and protect her.'

'True.'

'I'd like her for myself,' he suggested hopefully.

Zeus examined his son's face. It radiated happiness, and he could tell that Hermès had fallen in love with Pandora. This was a first for Hermès, as he had never shown this emotion before. In a monotone voice he explained, 'No, not you, I have other plans for her.'

Hermès looked hurt and disappointed. His face reddened and he became angry. He quickly settled as he knew there was no point trying to change Zeus' plans. Once they were made, he was oblivious to the needs and desires of others.

***

The following morning, Zeus returned to Heph's workshop without Hermès to meet with Pandora personally. He wanted to see for himself the progress that Pandora was making. He needed to be satisfied that she'd be the adequate representation of all future human females. He had learned that human males were now aware of her existence, and that they were enraptured at the prospect of her introduction into the human male population. If he liked her, he'd keep this one with the gods. One woman amongst so many human males would be dangerous for all of them, and especially for Pandora. He decided that she'd instrumental in pathfinding the future of the women's role in human societies. He was also confident that Athena had given this aspect much thought, and that she'd be planning to share her beliefs with him soon. She usually did.

He stepped into Heph's workshop without ceremony. Zeus was like that. He saw that Pandora was alone and he was pleased as his words were for her only. He approached her and reached out to hold her hand. She trembled as she offered it, but Zeus pretended not to notice. Many females trembled when he approached them.

'I believe you have found your voice,' he smiled as he asked gently, watching Heph and Athena entering the room.

'I have.' Pandora now looked toward Heph and Athena for support.

'Do you know who I am?' Zeus asked.

'You are Zeus, father to both Heph and Athena and you are King of the Gods,' she replied.

'Do you understand the idea of fathers and mothers? Zeus was now curious.

'I do,' she smiled. 'I hope to be a mother one day.'

Zeus hesitated responding. He considered the implications, finally he replied to her. 'I'm sure you will be, one day. What do you understand about the gods?'

'You are the creators of all things and are the rulers of everything. You have power over nature, and the elements, and you control human destinies. As the king of the gods, you are the leader and guide to all of the other gods,' she replied knowingly and continued. 'All of you have specialties, but your specialty, is the skies, winds, rain, thunder, and lightening.'

Zeus nodded, clearly impressed. 'You learn fast.'

Pandora smiled, aware that it was a compliment.

'I want you to meet the others. I want them to get to know you and for them to teach you many things,' Zeus explained.

'When will I be sent to live with the other humans?' she asked.

'That may never happen,' he answered kindly, but when he saw the look of dismay on her face, he quickly added the explanation. 'As the first human female, you'll be considerably outnumbered by the males. This will cause problems for them, as they are unrefined simple men. Already your teachings and abilities have surpassed them. They will lust for you and compete fiercely for your affections and your body. This could lead to them into doing physical harm to you, and each other. We don't want that. Your life will be here with the gods and goddesses.'

Pandora looked crestfallen, but Zeus could tell that she'd quickly resign herself to her fate. 'I'll find you a husband,' he told her, but she immediately looked alarmed. 'One that will comfort, protect, and guide you,' he added, hoping that his reassurance would settle her anxiety.

'Will he love me?'

'Of...,' he hesitated, then continued. 'It depends on how you treat him.'

'I don't understand.'

'Emotions are most often mirrored. If you seem happy toward someone, they'll more than likely behave happily towards you. If you are angry, then they'll reflect that anger back at you. If you are loving and kind, then they'll mirror your behaviour and they'll be loving and kind in return. It is important to take the initiative and remain in control of your situation.'

'What if they were in an angry mood before you meet them, does being happy change them?'

'It depends if you were the cause of their anger. Being happy when someone is angry with you, can amplify their mood, not reverse it. But if their anger is with someone else, then by you being sympathetic, you will calm them. You may also be in a position to help them with their problem, and thus increasing their loyalty toward you. Being a respected and a trusted problem solver is a powerful quality to have.'

Pandora said nothing. She was being bombarded with a massive volume of life skills. So far, she was understanding them, but she now feared becoming overwhelmed.

Zeus remained quiet. He sensed Pandora was slowly coming to terms with his words of wisdom. He was pleased with himself, and his explanation.

'I...' Pandora started to speak to break the silence, but hesitated.

'You should rest. Soon you'll be meeting the other gods and goddesses, and they'll want to get to know you, and they too will want to pass on to you the benefits of their wisdom. It'll be a busy day for you.'

Zeus watched her settle backwards onto the lounge chair, appearing to do as he bid. He smiled, nodded his head, and then exited.

***

The next day, Hermès visited Pandora once more. Heph and Athena were with her and Athena had commenced her training in needlework and weaving. He smiled, clearly pleased with her progress as she demonstrated her dexterity and enthusiasm. The pile of completed garments was growing. 'She's a quick learner, Hermès,' Athena explained praising Pandora.

'Good for you, Pandora,' Hermès encouraged. 'I've been tasked with adding to her word knowledge,' he explained. Athena nodded, knowing that it would be Zeus' command and she agreed that skills in language use was vital for her newly made friend. Hermès was an obvious tutor of these skills as he was the god responsible for developing the written word. She stood up and headed toward the door. 'I'll leave you both to it,' she announced as she departed.

Heph also realised that they needed to be alone, but as it was his workshop, he decided it shouldn't be him to have to leave. 'Why don't you walk while you talk,' he suggested. 'You could give Pandora her first tour of the city whilst explaining language craft to her.'

'An excellent suggestion,' Hermès agreed. 'Fresh air, exercised muscle's, stimulating sights, and great conversation. What more could a woman want?' he laughed.

So, arm in arm, Hermès and Pandora headed out through the door and into the sunlight.

'What did you want to teach me?' she asked.

'I want to teach you the indicators of when others are lying or being deceitful toward you. Humans, and especially gods and goddesses can be tricksters, and in their rage, jealousy, and cruelty, they can do you great mental harm.'

'Now, I'm scared.'

He laughed gently. 'That is why I'm here. I'm here to help you thwart them, and to teach you how you can thrive in a tough world.'

As they walked, she leaned into him, snug under his arm, feeling safe and cared for. She wanted to learn as much as he would teach her.

Hermès glowed happily as he realised that they were now becoming close friends. He suddenly remembered that he could never have her, and he stiffened and moved her away from their embrace. He cleared his throat, indicating that the lessons were now commencing. Pandora took his cue and she became attentive. She sensed his teachings would shape her life, and therefore her confidence and happiness.

'The first thing to master is knowing that there are two types of utterings. The first type is collaborative and this means that the conversation and its purpose is mutually beneficial. The second type is commanding and its purpose is to get other people to do for you what you want them to do. It may not be beneficial for both, but it will certainly be beneficial for the one giving the command. The technique here is to get in early. When you meet someone, quickly take charge. Discuss in detail what you want, and when you want it. Let them know that you'll be disappointed in them, or even angry with them if they let you down. In my experience, adopting a commanding role early in your dealings with others will always benefit you. If you don't, you may be cursed with doing their bidding, which may very well be unpleasant.'

'So, my happiness comes from taking charge and thereby getting what I want.'

'Exactly.' Hermès was enamoured. She was clearly an apt student. 'The second thing that you should become exceptionally skilled at, is to know how to always give compliments. People like to hear good things about themselves, and when you are the one dispensing that kindness, they'll become more beholden and enamoured toward you. They'll grow to thrive on your flattery, and they'll feel sad if you don't feed it to them.'

'What if they don't deserve it?'

'Oh, it doesn't need to be genuine. You can use whatever words you need, in order to get them on your side. Seduce them with your flattery and kindness, making them want more. You need to sound benevolent, but that is just to put them at ease as you take them more under your control. When you see that they are disappointed when not being praised, you'll know that you have them under your command. Zeus does this to everyone all the time. He is the master of manipulation, and look at him, he lives a great life.'

'So, as long as I appear gracious, and have them thrive on my flattery, they'll be under my power and want to do my bidding.'

'Sounds great, doesn't it?'

'Zeus warned me that I would be greatly outnumbered by the human males and that they will become greedy to know me and even want to own me. I need these powers you are teaching me to protect myself,' Pandora concluded.

'Many males are egotistical, and lustful, and will seek to dominate any females within their periphery,' Hermès agreed. 'They may also become competitive, and possibly combative, if challenged by others for your affections, regardless of your own feelings toward them.'

'I feel some trepidation, but also elation,' Pandora confessed.

'Kill trepidation,' Hermès advised. 'Confidence is king, let it rule you.'

Together, they walked past the many palaces and homes of the various gods and goddesses that lived at Mount Olympus. Many waved a friendly greeting to them, but Hermès responded without introduction. He was enjoying tutoring her and was pleased that she was she was a quick learner. They stopped at a water fountain and he invited her to drink, and then he took some water for himself. All this talking was thirsty work.

They rounded a corner and continued their unhurried tour, as they walked into a large grassy area which was bordered with pink, red, purple, and white flowering plants that were in full bloom. The trees and the garden beds were magnificent and Pandora gasped, fully appreciating the splendour.

They sat together on a park bench holding hands and Hermès continued the lesson. 'The third item on the list to learn is indifference. Other people's issues, worries, and problems, are of no concern to you, even if you caused them to happen.' Hermès studied Pandora's face for a reaction.

'My worries, issues, and problems, are my priorities, not their concerns, issues, or problems. Let them fend for themselves.' She smiled delighted with her new discovery.

'Good. Yes, excellent. You do learn fast.'

'I do strongly feel that as I'm outnumbered by everyone else, a girl needs to learn how to look out for herself,' Pandora agreed and she looked happy.

'The rule with indifference is to know how to show concern without actually feeling it, or doing anything to help them.'

'So, I don't tell them that I'm indifferent to their dilemma?'

'Never. You can offer a suggestion, or an opinion, but be sure you distance yourself from the outcome.'

'What else do I need to know?'

Hermès stood up from the park bench and held out his hand to assist Pandora, but she stood up by herself. He laughed.

In rapid fire, he listed the other qualities that would be of much value to her. 'Never raise your voice, especially in anger. Elevated voices reveal to others that you are fearful of losing control of the situation. You will appear weak and desperate. Next, never admit to making a mistake. If you do, never apologise. It's not your job to make amends, let them fix their own problems. Keep a record of everyone's mistakes, misdeeds, and weaknesses. List their darkest secrets and when the opportunity presents itself, only hint at your knowledge of them and the power you have over them.'

'But I can't read or write yet,' Pandora said sounding concerned.

Hermès cupped her eyes. He next held her hands. 'Now, you can read and write,' he explained as he smiled. 'We'll get you some papyrus and ink for you to practice with.'

Pandora was feeling overwhelmed. All these new skills, and all this new knowledge was happening so rapidly to her. She took in a deep breath. 'I think I'll need to rest soon.'

'Let me finish the lessons, and then you can sleep at my home. I will take good care of you.'

She leaned forward and hugged him. Hermès felt that his protegee was advancing her skill sets quickly and competently, and felt elated about what he was doing for her. She was a natural at this. He hadn't thought to teach her the power of a female hug over others, and yet, here she was doing it spontaneously to him.

'Teach me more,' she commanded as she leaned back and pressed her hips toward him.

He broke away from her. He felt his pangs of desire grow for her, but he also knew Zeus would never allow their union. He feared Zeus more than he was willing to risk progressing his lustful feelings and desires for this magnificent woman.

Hermès continued teaching. 'You must be contradictory about everything. Always use rational argument to keep them unbalanced and off-side. Let them feel weak and confused, and have them believe that you are strong. If you don't have an answer, be evasive, deflect the conversation toward something that you can control knowledge-ably, and if possible, bedazzle them.'

She nodded.

'If ever, on that rare occasion, that you feel that you must capitu-late, then make it seem like it was your plan to do so all along any-way. Explain that you were playing a game with them, or sharing an amusement, and that it was your intention to do it this other way all along.' He paused but she indicated that he must continue. 'Learn everything, become wise. Wisdom is power to use over others. Your skills and knowledge will make them more dependent on you, but, and this is important, never accept payment of any sort. They must, at all times, remain obligated to you.'

Hermès was slightly concerned that he was over doing all this advice. Yet, he was also pleased with himself that these lessons came from him so fluidly. He felt elated at being able to list off these qualities and to have such a deeply felt understanding of the ramifications and benefits for her, and importantly, for himself. She would now know how to protect herself and he was pleased to be the one teaching her.

'Always remember to never share your secrets with anyone.'

'What do I do if someone know something bad about me?' Pandora was concerned.

'If they tell you that they do, then tell them something even worse about them. Neutralise any power they have over you, by having even more power over them. Firstly, make the bad all about them, so you can dismiss what they know about you, as trivial. Deflect their evil words and intentions back onto them. If you can't do it about them, then make it about other people that they really care about.'

'I will.' Pandora nodded her understanding.

'But safety first. Everything you do, and think, must always remain your secret. Trust no-one, but yourself,' Hermès concluded.

'What about you?' she asked coyly.

He hugged her. 'You can always trust me,' he assured her holding her tightly. He broke free from her, 'The last thing I can think off right now, although I'm sure I'll think of more to teach you later, is that you must abandon friendships before they abandon you. If the relationship is becoming sour, or you feel you are losing your control and influence over them, then dismiss them. Cut them off quickly. Be bold about it and if you can, make it formal, and unequivocal. If they come back begging, then only accept them on your terms. If they don't, you must discredit them quickly and publicly before they can speak ill of you. Get in first, so that in their telling of the story, it makes them seem pitiful, or even revengeful, and leaves the hearer with a sour disbelieving feeling. Other people are a resource, keep them near to you only whilst they have value. Distance yourself from those that don't, or won't, contribute to your goal achievement.'

'What are my goals?' she was puzzled.

'To be strong, confident, to grow in reputation as an important person, to have their respect and for them to do work for you and be happy to do so. You want to be on the receiving end of life's riches, not the giving.'

When they reached Hermès' home, they entered together. He motioned for her to make herself comfortable on a sofa, whilst he poured her some wine. He offered it toward her, but she hesitated after sniffing the contents of the cup. 'It's called wine. As a refreshment, it has little value, but as a social lubricant, it is without equal. Mastering this drink will allow you greater control over others.'

'Should I drink it?'

'You should avoid it. Clean water will satisfy all your liquid needs. Wine is the juice from grapes which has been fermented into a strong, pungent, and weakening elixir that is consumed by many in large volumes. For the gods of Mount Olympus, it takes a lot of wine and a relaxed environment for the effects to give any influence. But with humans, one or two cups weakens their thinking and resistance.

By avoiding wine, when others are becoming weakened through consuming it, you will have the upper hand in any situation.'

'Why are you teaching me this?'

'When combined with the other things I have taught you, it solidifies your control over others. You do remember the lessons?' he queried.

Pandora smiled. She proceeded to perfectly paraphrase all the things that they had discussed.

Hermès' was extremely proud of her.

***

Unbeknown to Hermès and Pandora, Zeus had been observing these lessons. He was originally concerned that Hermès might try to seduce her and woo her for himself. His superior hearing overheard the lessons that Hermès instructed her on, and whilst he didn't find any fault with the actual content, he was concerned with the practical applications of the material. Zeus himself utilised these power skills over others, and he thought himself clever to do so. Essentially, he acknowledged that Pandora was a stranger in a strange land and would need all the assistance that the immortals could give her. What concerned him, was these skills would set her too far apart from the humans. She could destroy them and therefore she could never really be one of them.

He also knew that now, more than ever, that he did not want for her to experience coitus with Hermès.

Zeus hadn't yet determined if he wanted Pandora for himself. Sex with an attractive human woman was an important item on his list of things to do, but he wasn't sure it should be with the first woman of all creation. Besides, Hera would know, and she was already huffy with the prospect. For now, he wanted Pandora to remain pure, untouched, and unsullied.

He had instructed Promethius to commence replicating her female form, and now many human females were already emerging and integrating quickly into human society. They all had a similar shape to Pandora with variations to her in facial features, height, hair colour, and weight distribution. The process was being carried out without fuss or grandeur, and the male reaction to having female companionship was predictably positive and receptive.

He didn't hesitate when he arrived at Hermès front door. It wasn't locked and he didn't knock. He entered the palace with accustomed confidence and arrogance. He hesitated, as though he felt some trepidation that he might catch them in the act of coitus. He was a little surprised when he discovered them fully clothed, and seated next to each other at a table. Before them were unfurled scrolls, parchments, ink, and a writing quill.

Hermès and Pandora looked at Zeus without surprise. 'I'm teaching her how to read and write,' he explained, smiling.

Zeus motioned that he wanted to see her skills and so she offered her lettering to him. He was impressed as it was perfect.

***

Zeus helped himself to a cup of wine and relaxed with its contents on a sofa. Pandora and Hermès shared a secret smile. After a while, he got bored listening to Hermès monotone voice issuing writing techniques about style, spelling, and sentence structure. 'I want both of you to continue this lesson later,' he bellowed.

Pandora looked up from her work as if startled by the interruption. Hermès was surprised, and slightly amused that he hadn't interrupted earlier. 'Do you need Pandora for something?' he asked, feigning interest.

'I want her to spend some time with Aphrodite. You are excellent at teaching Pandora many things Hermès, but the art of being female is Aphrodite's domain,' Zeus explained.

Hermès took the announcement in his stride as he had anticipated it. He motioned to Pandora to stand up and to go with Zeus to be with Aphrodite. He was pleased that their non-verbal communication skills were working so well when she had imperceptibly nodded her understanding and acceptance.

Zeus led Pandora and they exited the building and walked casually to Aphrodite's palace. They talked about what she had learned so far and Zeus was confident that they were preparing her well for life amongst the gods and goddesses.

Aphrodite didn't appear surprised when Zeus and Pandora casually entered her home. Zeus had little respect for other people's personal space. She quickly surmised that Pandora was here for tuition or guidance. She immediately approved of her involvement, and so she smiled at Pandora, welcoming her into her home, and her life.

Zeus studied them both together. 'Teach her the art of being female,' he instructed as he turned and exited the building.

Aphrodite turned to face her new charge. 'What do you know so far?' she asked.

Pandora spent some time paraphrasing, yet again, the lessons that Hermès had imparted on her. If Aphrodite was impressed, she didn't show it. She shrugged and nodded in agreement that his initial preparation of her had been adequate.

'To be a strong confident woman takes much more than controlling others to get what you want. When a woman has uncompromising beauty, such as yourself, it becomes a valuable asset that you must learn to control. Giving your heart and body to another without first securing benefits is a waste. You are most desirable, and therefore you are entitled to a great life,' Aphrodite explained.

Pandora looked about her, trying to imagine her beauty as an asset. Aphrodite looked at her with interest. 'Disrobe,' she commanded.

The dress that Athena had made for her, was so far the only clothing she had ever worn. Pandora didn't feel self-conscious about her body, so she readily complied. She flicked the clothing off her shoulders and it fell to her feet. She casually stepped out of it, and using one foot she flung it off the floor and onto the couch. Aphrodite observed Pandora's nakedness and wasn't unimpressed. Her body was perfectly proportioned, and her body hair was minimal and discrete. Importantly, she didn't feel challenged, or threatened by her either. Aphrodite decided that she would help this woman, and thereby maintain both her power and control over her. Crucially, she would manage the manner and nature of Pandoras future sexual liaisons as Aphrodite abhorred competition.

'I will now teach you grace, poise, and the art of sexually pleasuring a man. She left the chamber and returned with a simple day dress for Pandora to wear and offered it to her. She looked at it, examined it, and then put it on without comment. She next followed Aphrodite into the adjoining room. It was furnished with day beds, sofas, and soft cushions which depicted scenes of naked people performing various sexual acts. Along one side of the room was a table with food and wine. Aphrodite motioned for Pandora to help herself to some. Pandora looked at the offering. 'Is there any water? I don't drink wine,' and she looked at Aphrodite and was surprised to see her smiling.

'Do you want to have children?' Aphrodite asked her charge.

'I don't know yet. I haven't seen or met any to know what they are like,' Pandora replied.

'Children are smaller versions of ourselves. You feed them food and ideas and they grow up to be much like their parents. For the gods this process is accelerated and our children grow rapidly into adult form. For large animals however, they seem to take a long time to grow into adult size. All parents, especially females, seem to be burdened with feeding, training, and caring for them for a long time, and so I'm sure it'll be the same burden on all human women.'

'What benefit do they bring to our lives?'

'Not much, from what I can tell. But without them, our numbers would eventually decrease and there would be fewer of us to have fun with.'

'They do seem tiresome. Why do you ask me about children?'

'They are. I don't have any yet, but I'm sure I'll push some brats into the world one day. Hopefully, they'll add value to my life.'

'Why are we talking about them?'

'Men are cursed with their incessant desire to have sex. They are driven to it as if pushed by some unseen force that weakens their mind and makes them exceedingly pliable to the whims of the woman who use sex to control him. The more gorgeous the woman, the stronger they desire her. However, one of the possible side effects of sex with a man is pregnancy. Much can be achieved when your man is aroused, and he must be allowed to eventually ejaculate, or he'll become frustrated, and his mind will turn to rage. It is a finely tuned balancing act. I will teach you how to enjoy sex, and especially how to use the promise of sex to get more of what you want, but you do put yourself at risk of getting pregnant,' Aphrodite explained.

'That's easy. I won't have sex...,' Pandora concluded. She hesitated but then added, 'unless I decide that I do want to have children. I don't know about that yet.'

'Oh, my dear, you do want to have sex. It is the most wonderful thing two or more people can do with their bodies. When you are in the moment, all of Mount Olympus could burn and you wouldn't know it, or even care. A climax during sex is everyone's goal. Multiple orgasms are a bonus and I'll teach you how to achieve them. You'll want sex for the pleasure it gives you. Most of all, you'll want the power you'll achieve over the males due to their desire for sharing a sexual romp with you. They'll willingly submit to your control over them, and even surrender much of their decision making. The more they desire you, the weaker their minds become.'

'Now, I am intrigued. Tell me more.'

'The art of being a woman is to use the allure of your sex appeal to entice men to do your bidding. For this you must dress in clean, colourful clothing that reveals much but not everything. You must rid yourself of offensive odours, and then add subtle perfumes that excite them. Jewellery attracts men's attention, so wear some, but not too much as it quickly becomes boring.' Aphrodite paused her lesson to gauge Pandora's comprehension of what she was explaining. When she was satisfied that she was keeping up, she continued. 'The sexiest feature of any woman, is her voice. The seductive words she speaks are first to entice, and then ensnare him. When combined with a soft pitch used to deliver them, it renders any man into willing submission. You can describe in detail all manner of sexual fantasies as that will make them more eager. You don't have to do them, as it is only the illusion of the promise that binds them to you. Even just the hint of having sex with them, and the pleasures only you are willing give, are an incredibly strong motivator for males. Use it wisely so that they'll willingly agree to your needs, desires, and pleasures. I regard it as being, "the male curse," as they are quite powerless to resist be controlled.'

'What drives their curse?'

'Have you been introduced to male genitalia?'

'No, not yet, but I am curious.'

'I thought you might be,' Aphrodite giggled. 'They are so much fun,' she squealed in delight. Aphrodite walked over to the buffet motioning Pandora to follow her. Men have a penis which is shaped much like this sausage, she held one up to demonstrate, and next laid it on the table. Below the penis are two ball shaped bits that are held together in a sack of skin.' She next placed two meatballs on either side of the end of the sausage. 'When a man gets excited, his penis swells to twice its size.' She grabbed a larger sausage and replaced the smaller one to demonstrate. 'When that happens, all he can think about is putting it inside of you and ejaculating.'

'Inside of me!' Pandora was alarmed. 'Where?'

'Inside the cleft between your legs,' Aphrodite explained. 'Don't worry, as long as you are in control of it, sex is a wonderful experience and highly desirable, if not a tiny bit messy when they come. However, if you surrender control of it, it can be ugly and painful. The secret of being a powerful woman is to use the promise of sex to get men to do what you want, and then to enjoy having that sex with them on your terms. Don't ever let the men force you into having sex, as you'll feel violated, and that will be an awful outcome for you.'

'Why are men so obsessed with sex?'

'They can't help it,' Aphrodite explained. 'Their balls, or testes, produce chemicals that affect their brain. Remove them and they become docile and disinterested, so they are absolutely no fun in bed,' Aphrodite laughed. 'The threat of cutting them off whilst they sleep makes them wince,' she laughed again. 'With them attached, they are seemingly permanently aroused, and so they are constantly seeking opportunities to express their lust and desires. Depending on your mood, this can be either a redeeming quality, or an exasperating prospect.'

'It must be exhausting for them,' Pandora concluded.

'Males think they keep their lust a secret. They think we don't know they are desperately seeking out and revealing at the sight of our exposed skin. They try to imagine what we look like naked. They like to believe that they are discreet about it, but all experienced women know their truth. All women know to who, and how much of ourselves that we are revealing. We enjoy the effect it has on them and we treat it as a compliment. We'd actually be disappointed if they weren't looking at us.

'I don't like it.'

'You'll lead a happier and more fulfilled life if you accept it, and master managing it. Look, all males are lustful, and when they talk about their male needs among themselves, they describe it in some kind of secretive brotherhood code. We women happily tolerate their juvenility about sex, so long as when it does happen, that it is on our terms.'

'Don't they think about anything else?'

'Oh, most of the time they can behave themselves and carry out their normal tasks. But their switch toward arousal is never hard to find, and once they are erect, it's somewhat difficult to turn them off without giving them an ejaculation. The thing is to use this switch to your advantage. It is even better when you complete this without the male realising that you are doing it to them. Once you have a hold of them, it is simply a matter of maintaining that control, and they'll do almost anything on the promise of reciprocated physical affections.

They are often silly about it, sometimes amusing, and occasionally hilarious in that way.'

'They are willingly cursed by their own balls,' Pandora concluded pointing to the demonstration model on the table.

'Especially the younger adult males,' Aphrodite agreed. 'Maturity brings some rationality, charm, and much more attentiveness to the act.'

'You prefer older males?'

'I prefer experienced males. The young ones are an interesting diversion, an amusement, but it is all over too soon. To enjoy great sex, go for an experienced male every time.'

'What about, love?'

'Love is okay, but power is everything. Let the males fall deeply in love with you, and should you feel charitable, you can tell them that you love them in return. A woman's love is always conditional to the benefits that the male can provide her.'

'Teach me more.' Pandora now wanted this power over men. To not have it seemed irresponsible, and Aphrodite clearly knew what she was doing. She now realised that she was extremely fortunate to have her as her tutor and mentor.

'When a commanding male is pursuing you for sex, you can often neutralise his passion by submitting to it as if it was a boring thing to do, and that the two of you should just get it over and done with. Powerful males crave the pursuit, they are hunters and they see us as their prey. Give in easily, and they'll lose the thrill of the chase. Your easy submission and declared boredom with the impending act of copulation with them, will quickly deflate their ardour.'

'And their penis,' Pandora added.

They laughed.

For the next seven days and nights, the two women delved deeper into what it was to be female. Aphrodite the teacher, was greatly enjoying the engagement and she discovered that it helped her with a clearer understanding of her own feminine power. They discussed all aspects of intercourse including taboos and other ugly aspects of sex that were best avoided. Aphrodite also covered topics that included preventing unwanted pregnancies, feminine hygiene, intimate grooming, prolonging the intimacy, the benefits of sexual fantasy, how to set the scene for intimacy, using body language effectively, the creation and wearing of alluring costumes, and Aphrodite's personal favourite, all about achieving multiple orgasms.

Aphrodite also spent some time discussing female competition, and the bitchiness that other jealous women can exhibit, when they realise that you have more power over their men than they do, especially if they think your baiting their husband.

Pandora the student was now growing so much in confidence that she could not only control men, but that she could also now comfortably deflect any ill intent demonstrated by other women who'd might feel threatened by her.

They also reiterated the lessons that Hermès gave her. Aphrodite could find no fault in them, but added one feature. That the power of alliances should not be underestimated. They agreed that two women protecting each other's backs would have tremendous benefits. Their relationship with each other must be total and unconditional, as deceiving each other would be their downfall, and that would be emotionally painful and cause permanent bitterness. They also agreed that there were enough men out there for them to share them out. They'd never compete with each other for a male, as they were theirs to divide and conquer.

Aphrodite was satisfied. She now believed she had complete and absolute control over Pandora.

***

On the seventh day of Pandora's feminine wile's tuition, Zeus arrived at Aphrodite's palace to check on her progress. Pandora noted that Aphrodite didn't seem surprised and thought perhaps that she'd expected him. They welcomed him in and Pandora fussed over him by serving him tasty foods, pouring him generous cups of wine, and complimenting him on his looks and prowess. He enjoyed the attention and Pandora thought she sensed she may have gained some control over the god king. But she soon realised that she was mistaken, whilst he enjoyed the attention, the food, and drink, he wasn't tempted by either her beauty or her charms. Pandora was both concerned and saddened by her poor performance. Aphrodite took Pandora into another room and consoled her. 'Zeus is unlike normal males. He is a poor test subject. It'll be much easier with a human man or a simpler god.'

Pandora forced a smile and the two returned to the main room. Zeus was standing. He explained the purpose of his visit. 'It is now time for Pandora to leave your palace, Aphrodite. Her lessons with you are clearly complete. You are ready to move on to the next phase of your introduction to life amongst the gods and goddesses.'

The two women hugged with Pandora whispering a thank you. Pandora next followed Zeus out of the building.

They walked in silence for a while, and then Pandora asked, 'Where are we going?'

'My palace. The other gods and goddesses are assembled there, and they want to meet you. They have some gifts to give you,' Zeus explained.

'I have learned that you are married,' Pandora said to the god king.

'Yes, I'm married to Hera,' Zeus admitted. 'Heph is my son and it was I that arranged for him to create you as the first human woman.'

'Am I exceeding your expectations?' Pandora asked hopefully.

'Yes, and from your form, many new women are now being created and are now being successfully integrated into the human world.'

'Will they all have the benefits of my learning and training?' Pandora asked feeling concerned for them.

Zeus had pondered Pandora's fate. He remembered that Hera had warned him to stay away from Pandora and not to be tempted to bed her. Even though she had truly exceeded his expectations, he had conceded that this experiment had failed and that it was his fault. He had allowed her training to go too far. She was a great design, but now too clever for the human world. She was strong willed, confident, and too knowledgeable to be an effective intellectual prototype for all other human women. They needed to be as base and simple as their male counterparts. Having more like Pandora would demoralise and ultimately destroy mankind. He decided that she would spend her life amongst the gods and goddesses. He also concluded that she needed to be married, and had given it some thought as to who it should be with. He needed to be some inconsequential God, so that their union would remove her from the general population, and that would reduce her influence.

He looked at her and answered her question, 'No, you are unique in this way. I believe that your future life will be here with the gods on Mount Olympus, and not with the humans.'

They continued walking without further discussion. Pandora was also pondering her fate. She was about to meet the gods and goddesses of Mount Olympus' high society. The impression she made on them would affect their behaviours and attitudes toward her, all women, and humans generally for many years to come.

When they arrived at the palace, Pandora was amazed at the number of gods and goddesses that were assembled to meet her. It seemed that there were too many to count. She followed Zeus two steps behind him, remembering her lessons that their king was to be feared, respected, obeyed, and never underestimated.

Zeus was already becoming bored with the process. Many gasped in delight upon seeing Pandora. She was stunningly beautiful and dressed resplendently in a full-length, glittering gold coloured dress that show her cleavage to full advantage. Pandora was taught that her perfect breasts were an asset and that she should be proud to display them to full effect over others. Her long, perfectly formed legs were also an asset. Her magnificent long shiny hair flowed in her wake as she smiled generously at Zeus's guests that had now come forward to meet her.

Zeus sat heavily on his throne and motioned to his daughter, Hebe to bring him some wine. Zeus spotted his human male servants eyeing Pandora with interest. "She is way too much for you boys", he thought to himself.

The expansive room was filled with many guests. Some had plans to personally meet with Pandora and there seemed to be some organisation as to the protocols they were to observe. There were many tables lining the room filled with exotic foods and goblets brimming with wine. Guests unhurriedly picked at the food and sample the drink, focusing their attention on the new comer, Pandora, a simple human living among the gods and goddesses of Mount Olympus.

Hephaestus was the first to come forward to greet Pandora. She knew him and so smiling happily, threw her arms around him in a familiar embrace. She hadn't yet thanked him for her life and wished to publicly do so now. Heph was pleased with her exuberance and smiled happily in return. Their extended embrace was observed by all, and some wondered about the nature of their relationship.

When they moved apart, Heph revealed his gift to her. 'I have fashioned this writing quill for you, Pandora. You can use it to record all the words of wisdom that you learn, and you can use it to plan for the dreams and wishes that you want to come true. Oh, you can also use it to record your thoughts and then send them to someone special by courier. In this way you can communicate with others no matter how far away they are.'

Pandora examined the quill. It was fashioned with gold and silver leaf. It had sufficient weight so as to feel it, and to be able to use it purposely, but still light enough so as not to tire the writer. 'Thank you Heph, I'll use it with love as you intended.'

Next came Athena. She was also well known to Pandora and so they also embraced with delightful enthusiasm. 'I also have a gift for you,' she explained. 'I grant you the power to control your fears, and to never feel despair,' Atheana explained smiling benevolently.

Pandora was wise enough to recognise the value of this gift and she showed her gratitude with another hug. 'Thank you,' she whispered.

The next goddess that came forward was Zeus' wife, Hera. She was feeling stiff and starchy about Pandora's existence, and was clearly not in favour of human women being so beautiful and alluring. Hera had previously expressed her concerns to Zeus who seemingly accepted that Pandora wasn't going to be added to his list of sexual conquests. She knew it wasn't an easy promise for Zeus to make, as she believed he felt an overwhelming desire to have her. 'Hello Pandora. I am Hera, wife of Zeus and Queen of the Goddesses. My gift to you, one which I believe you'll welcome, is relief from exhaustion. I believe that human women will ultimately be required to perform many tasks. Your burden will be great and much will be expected of all women. My gift will give you, and to all other women, the strength and perseverance to carry on, to power through any exhaustion, despite already having accomplished so much.'

'Thank you, Hera, your gift is both thoughtful and appreciated. I can now understand why Zeus tells me he is such a fortunate man to have you as his wife. You are gorgeous, wise, and intelligent. I believe that we can become great friends and share many wonderful and ful-filling adventures together.'

Hera studied her. Pandora sounded sincere, but Hera was easily suspicious so she simply smiled her reply, she nodded her acknowl-edgment, and then slowly withdrew returning to the others.

The next goddess to step forward was Persephone, wife of Hades, God of the underworld. 'Greetings Pandora, she smiled and offered her hand in friendship. 'My name is Persephone. My husband, Hades and I rule the underworld.'

'How fascinating,' Pandora responded looking pleased to meet her. 'I gather we all end up enjoying the pleasure of your company in the underworld one day?' She smiled sweetly as if this was a positive event and one that she should look forward to experiencing.

'Not for the immortals, but certainly for all humans. Hermès has told me a great deal about you. I think he is your number one admirer.' Persephone lowered her voice and continued. 'Be careful, I think he may have plans to seduce you.'

Pandora gushed like an immature young woman. 'Oh, I'd be so for-tunate and happy to be all his. He is a delightful and a wonderful god and has taught me so many valuable things. I really wouldn't be the woman I am today without his mentoring, love, and support.'

'I believe Aphrodite has been guiding you also?' Persephone queried.

'She has, but I feel she may have some additional agendas, and not just my future well-being at heart. I'm sure that you can speak knowledgeably about Aphrodite's character. I look forward to carrying on our conversation at a more private venue,' Pandora added conspiratorially.

'I also look forward to that opportunity,' Persephone replied. She was impressed with this human woman. Clearly, she has the skill set to survive among immortals. She wondered how she'd fair among the humans. 'My gift to you is simple but valuable. As a mortal, your death is inevitable. My gift to you is the power to acknowledge your fate, and the realisation that you shouldn't fear death. You must not be saddened by the prospect of dying, as when you do die, you'll be transported to a better place to be with me and my husband.' She smiled.

Pandora was quick to demonstrate her understanding of the benefit of her gift. 'You have given me the confidence that I need to live a full and happy life, knowing that I will be loved, wanted, and cared for, in my afterlife with you. I cherish you for your thoughtfulness, and I hope that we can become great friends.' Pandora ensured that she positively radiated her delight at this gift.

Persephone smiled awkwardly in return, feeling unsure how to respond to her. So, she too just smiled her reply, nodded her acknowledgment, and slowly withdrew to return to the others.

Demeter was next to step forward and walk to Pandora. She didn't offer her hand in greeting and stopped just short of where Pandora was standing. The lack of warmth that Demeter displayed was clearly obvious to Pandora, so she tactfully reached forward and embraced the Goddess. Demeter was stunned, but equally resolved not to show her surprise. She gently broke away from the embrace and faced Pandora.

Pandora was smiling effusively. 'You are Demeter, one of the most important goddesses in all the world,' Pandora announced.

Demeter was a bit taken back with Pandora's pronouncement. 'Oh, um, I wouldn't say that,' was all she managed to reply.

'You are the Goddess of the harvest and therefore the bringer of food. I have sampled much of it in my short life here among you all. Food gives life, and the clever and interesting ways it is prepared, makes eating it a delightful experience. We all have much to be grateful for all that you do for us,' she explained adding a generous smile.

Demeter was taken aback. No one had ever taken her contribution so seriously before. She was used to just providing the harvest. She took great pride and care in her role, but she was accustomed to being the quiet achiever.

Pandora broke the silence between them. 'Aren't you also the mother of Persephone?'

'Yes! I am,' she replied pointing to her daughter who was mingling with the other gods and goddesses.

'She is fortunate to have you as her mum. Sadly, I'll never experience the bond with a mother like the one that you have with your daughter.' Pandora looked crestfallen.

Demeter's resolve weakened. She was previously determined to remain indifferent with Zeus' experiment. She was here to present her gift, and then planned to discreetly exit the gathering. But Pandora was different. She was intelligent, strong, and confident. She displayed a maturity exceeding many others that she dealt with. She wasn't sure how to categorise her feelings toward this human woman so she did the next best thing, she hugged her.

Pandora melted into the embrace. She had won her over and she was delighted with herself.

Demeter withdrew from her hold. She became aware that everyone in the room, including her daughter Persephone, was staring at them. She stiffened and spoke formally. 'My gift to you, Pandora, is the freedom from the anxiety of being hungry. There will always be fruits, crops, and animals to harvest for their food. It shall be plentiful, tasty, and nutritious. Live your life knowing you will always have food on your table.'

'Mother, may I join you?' The voice was from a younger God who approached Demeter and Pandora.

Demeter smiled and turned to the male god who approached them. She proudly introduced him to Pandora. 'This is my son, Plutus. Like his sister and I, he also enjoys agriculture.'

Plutus smiled benevolently at Pandora. He turned to his mother, 'Please forgive the interruption mother, but I must depart soon, and I wanted to quickly introduce myself and give my gift to Pandora before I go.'

'Oh dear, have I taken too long with this popular girl.'

'No,' Pandora gushed. 'I really enjoy your company, and I especially love and appreciate your thoughtful gift,' Pandora explained radiating happiness.

'I too have a gift for you,' Plutus explained. 'My gift to you is the enjoyment of your life without ever experiencing poverty. The lands and its peoples will always provide you with the means to have enough of what you'll ever need, or want.'

'I'm humbled by your gift, Plutus. I thank you and so receive it graciously.' Pandora curtsied to indicate her humbleness.

Plutus reached out and lifted her face toward him. Demeter was concerned that they were about to kiss, but Plutus gently caressed her face. 'The bounty is yours, Pandora. Sometimes it will come easily, and sometimes you may need to earn it through hard work and toil. But as my mother can corroborate, the land provides us with everything we need for a happy life. Learn its secrets and enjoy the bounty,' Plutus explained. He next kissed his mother's cheek, bowed toward Pandora, and departed.

Apollo took this as an opportunity to come forward to present his gift. He grabbed his Aunt Demeter from behind and tickled her. Demeter turned to learn who it was that had assaulted her. 'Apollo, you know I don't like it when you do that!' she scolded.

'Sorry Aunty,' he tried to look apologetically, but his face radiated mischief. 'I really couldn't help myself,' he grinned.

'This is my nephew Apollo, and he must have a gift for you also,' Demeter concluded.

'I do!' Apollo looked pleased with himself.

'Then I shall leave you both to it,' Demeter explained. 'I'll take this opportunity to depart from you both, as I have places to visit and many things to do.' She studied Pandora. 'I wish you well my dear,' she said sincerely with a hint of sad foreboding. She leaned forward and hugged Pandora once more, then broke from the embrace, turned, and slowly walked away.

'Don't mind Aunty. She can seem a bit frumpy at times, but truly, she is the salt of the earth.'

'I thought salt was bad for the soil,' Pandora queried mischievously.

'Too much of it will kill all plants and all animals. But it is also true, that without a little bit of salt, we wouldn't have life at all.'

'Thank you for making that clearer for me to understand. You must be one of those rare, wise, and intelligent gods,' Pandora concluded.

'I sometimes manage to impress myself,' Apollo agreed cheekily.

'I do hope you have a gift for me that matches your talents,' she smiled as she challenged him.

Apollo smiled in return. He couldn't tell if she had just teased him, or had paid him a compliment. 'My gift for you is the remedy of illness and the prevention of injury. I bestow upon you a healthy life, and the means to cure all that ails you, and the skill to know how to repair your injuries.'

'I now feel complete. Your gift is both generous and beneficial. I'll accept it on one condition.'

Apollo was initially confused. He was wary of having conditions set upon him, especially when he was feeling so generous. 'Tell me your condition, and if it is within my power, I will do all I can to oblige you.'

'Teach me what you know of medicine and healing. Agree to have me as your pupil. Guide me on how to not only look after my own health, but how to help others with their health and well being also.'

Apollo's heart melted. Being a physician was all about caring for the health and welfare of others. This woman, the first of many, now wanted to share his passion for helping others cure their sickness and mend their wounds. 'I agree to your condition,' he replied, speaking calmly. He now felt he was in some awe of her, and the developmental progress she had clearly made, in the relatively short time since her creation. 'I would be proud to share my knowledge of healing with you.'

Pandora smiled, leaned forward, and gently kissed his cheek, wrapping her arms about him.

Apollo blushed. He felt the warmth of her body and the peak of her firm breasts against him as they embraced. She smelt amazing. He broke free, now aware of his impending arousal. He mumbled a farewell, turned, and left to return to the others to continue with eating and drinking and hopefully, be merry.

Pandora was delighted.

Next, three young women with colourful floral arrangements in their hair, seized the opportunity to swamp Pandora with their presence. They carried trays of food realising that Pandora hadn't been eating due to all of the fuss being made of her. They place the food trays on a nearby empty table. They surrounded her, all talking excitedly with hello's and so wonderful to meet you, and how are you enjoying yourself, and aren't all these gifts you're getting wonderful? You are so lucky.'

Pandora held up both hands to quell their excitement. 'You all look, and sound fabulous. Now please tell me who you all are,' she asked as scooped up some of the food and ate it hungrily.

'I'm, Aglaia,' she said cheerfully, radiating her happiness as she introduced herself. She held out her hand offering a limp wrist but playful handshake.

'I'm, Euphrosyne,' the second one explained. She too beamed, and grinned her merriment.

'And I am, Thalia,' the third one told her happily. I'm the life of the party,' she claimed as she bounced happily, clapping her hands.

'We're all the life of the party,' Aglaia added. We often hang out with Aphrodite, so we know all about you.'

Pandora smiled benevolently. 'So, I guess you already know, that I like to party also?'

'Oh, that's a relief. We hoped that you were a party girl. Some of the older goddesses are a bit starchy but when we get together with Aphrodite, Araes, and Dionysus, we all have the best time.'

'So much fun.'

'What qualities are you best known for?' Pandora asked showing interest in them.

'We're charming and we love to sing,' one claimed. 'And we're beautiful and we love to dance,' claimed another. 'We draw from nature to bestow creativity onto others,' concluded the third.

'Oh, and we're sisters. Our mum is Eurynome, and Zeus,' and they all turned to point him out, 'is our daddy, even though he never acts like it,' Aglaia explained. 'But we don't care very much because we like to party.'

Thalia explained. 'Some people call us the Three Graces and some call us the Charites,'

'Well, I would feel both grateful and fortunate to be able to call each of you my dear friends,' Pandora responded invitingly.

'Aww!' all three chorused. 'Of course we're your best friends. We love you.'

'The gifts!' one exclaimed remembering.

'We have gifts of jewellery for you which are all inspired by our love of the great outdoors,' another explained.

Thalia revealed a cloth roll which she laid carefully onto a nearby table and unfurled it in front of Pandora. The first item she picked up was a brooch. It was about the size of her palm. She held it up to the light and laughed happily. The centre spine of the brooch was a collection of rough-cut white diamonds. On either side of them were a mixture of emeralds and peridot gems. The brooch shimmered in the light and it looked much like a waterfall cascading out of a lush jungle setting.

'This is amazing,' Pandora gushed. She accepted the gift and also held it up to the light, bedazzled by the effect.

She gestured for Thalia to pin it on her and Talia responded gleefully. The three admired the jewellery now pinned to Pandoras chest, the weight of it pulling down on her top, now revealing more breast than she had previously revealed. No one cared.

'This one is my favourite,' Euphrosyne declared happily. The next piece was a wrist band made from blue sapphires and topaz gems. It was about the length of Pandora's middle finger. On the leading edge nearer her hand was masses of small yellow Citrine stones mixed in with small amber stones. She opened the clasp and indicated to Pandora to hold out her wrist. Pandora did so, and Euphrosyne placed the wrist band onto Pandora and clasped it secure. Pandora held it between them for all to see. The arrangement of stones was stunning.

'It symbolises where the ocean meets the sandy beach,' Euphrosyne explained.

The last piece of jewellery was Aglaia's creation. They looked at the necklace and admired the arrangement of emeralds, peridots, and rubies, held together by strands of gold chain in the shape of a tree. At its base was a long length of smoky brown quartz crystal representing the tree's trunk. Some thinner smoky brown quartz crystals were placed to represent major branches. Aglaia held it up against her own chest to demonstrate how it would look on Pandora.

Pandora was weeping from the pure happiness she now felt, and the three women chorused 'Aww.'

Talia moved forward to hug Pandora and she gratefully reciprocated. They next spun Pandora around and Talia clasped the necklace around her neck. Euphrosyne held up a mirror for Pandora to see herself wearing the ornate jewellery. The tree trunk sat neatly in Pandoras cleavage and her breathing gave the tree of life the appearance of movement as the gems caught the light.

Aglaia spoke in hushed tones. 'It symbolises the tree of life and it honours your part as the first human woman and your role in giving humanity a happier future.'

Hera had been watching the young woman's gift giving with interest. When she spotted the necklace, she became sufficiently intrigued and walked forcibly toward the four women, imposing herself onto their group. She closely examined the tree of life necklace and turned to the women, clearly fuming. 'I alone have the right to this symbol. This jewellery represents the same "tree of life" that my grandmother, Gaia gifted to me. You should not have this.'

'This is a different tree, Hera. See, it has red apples, not golden apples like yours,' Aglaia defended.

'You have the real tree in your garden, Hera. So, why do you concern yourself with this simple piece of jewellery,' Talia spoke urgently trying to defuse the situation. Hera could be spiteful and malicious when offended.

Hera looked at the necklace and then looked at the four women, each in turn. 'This is poorly constructed,' she concluded. 'It will fall apart the moment you walk. I recommend you take it off, and hide it amongst your other baubles.' Hera stood looking fierce. Getting no reaction from the others, she turned and walked hastily over to Zeus to complain.

It was now clear that the previous mood of cheerfulness had been replaced with gloom. No one spoke for an age, so when Pandora spoke it almost came as a surprise. 'I love my jewellery, and I especially love the three of you. These are wonderful gifts and I shall treasure them always.'

Aglaia, Talia, and Euphrosyne, each in turn hugged Pandora. Next, the three sisters held hands and skipped away, heading first to the refreshments, and then onto where Aphrodite, Araes, and Dionysus were seated in the company of several beautiful nymphs.

Pandora turned when she heard a woman's voice call her name. She saw Zeus' youngest daughter, Hebe, approaching her. 'I want to share some of my hard learned wisdom with you, Pandora,' Hebe explained. 'I'm sorry that I don't have much else to offer you, but I'm young compared to the others,' she explained as she looked toward the gathering who were observing them with interest.

'Your words of wisdom will be really appreciated, Hebe,' Pandora conceded with a generous smile.

Hebe laughed. 'The thing I always try to do, is to always give sincere and honest appreciation for everything that anyone does for me.'

'I appreciate you telling me that.'

'I do it to arouse in others, their desire to become more invested in my happiness.'

'A worthy trait to develop,' Pandora agreed.

'Be sure to only hint at what they should do to help you. It is important that they believe that it was their idea to do so, in the first place. Make it a little bit obvious that you are over dramatizing the problem, so that they get the point. Then apologise for doing so, so that they can come to your rescue.'

'You have really thought this through,' Pandora said and sounded impressed.

'Trust me. Letting them feel that they have ownership, and therefore a greater responsibility, to the solution to my problem works perfectly for me. I want them to feel happy that they are helping me. If I can, I make it seem like a challenge that they must master, as they put greater energy into the solution, and they'll get greater satisfaction when it works, and they are proven correct. It leaves them feeling very smart and pleased with themselves,' Hebe grinned.

'Interesting.'

'Lastly, you should never complain about your life, or criticise about how others are treating you. You should try to be upbeat about everything, all the time.'

'That may be a challenge,' Pandora conceded.

'A worthy endeavour. Trust me, it works. No one likes a sourpuss.'

You are both smart and clever, Hebe,' Pandora concluded.

'I have to be, Pandora, and so do you.' And with that, Hebe turned and departed Pandora's company.

The next god to come forth was Hermès. He skipped playfully toward her and scooped her up in his arms twirling her around the room playfully.

She laughed and kissed his cheek as he gently set her down. They embraced happily and with familiarity, under the gawking stares of all the others. Hermès next reached his arm about her waist and gently manoeuvred her well out of listening range of the others.

'Remember my dear, you must always do the following,' he started to explain.

Pandora looked concerned and worried she had somehow disappointed her mentor.

'Smile!' he reminded her. 'Whatever is happening, always smile sincerely.'

She smiled.

'And use the word "yes" as often as you can. If your answer is going to be "no", then stall before uttering it. Always delay the negative and reinforce the positive.'

She nodded and smiled.

'When being introduced, remember to immediately repeat back the other person's name as if it was the sweetest name that you have ever heard.'

'Okay, but you could have taught me that one sooner,' she observed.

Hermès grinned about his guilty omission. 'Only talk about the small mistakes that you have made, apologise sincerely for them, so that others will quickly defend and forgive you. In turn they'll become more willing to confide and trust in you. Showing a little fallibility goes a long way.'

'I understand.' She nodded.

'Always show genuine interest in the immortals. Compliment them in such a way so that they feel obliged to live up to your praise. Commend every improvement they make, no matter how trivial.'

'I've been doing that.'

'Be a great listener, show interest in what they are saying and behave as if you are enriched by the time and energy that they have spent with you. Make it all about them, and that they are important, valued, and respected. They are more important to you because of what they have done or plan to do.'

'I listen and I tell them I understand.'

'Good,' he paused to reflect. 'Only ask questions that are easily answered. Take the long route to learn about what you want or need and, in that way, people won't become suspicious of your motives.'

Pandora took a deep breath.

'Listen carefully. I believe that Zeus has plans to have sex with you. If he does, submit gracefully. It may not be all that pleasurable, but your role is to submit to wishes and desires of your king.'

Pandora said nothing. She tried to smile, but this time she failed. She felt weakened and desperately wanted to flee the room.

Aphrodite stepped forward and came closer to Pandora, completely blocking her from being seen by the others. She was effectively hiding the look of distress that was now clearly evident on Pandoras face.

'I warned her about Zeus' plans,' Hermès explained to Aphrodite.

'He is a beast of a male, and he'd be the last god I'd ever want to have sex with,' Aphrodite growled.

'You're not helping,' Hermès cautioned.

'Of course, you must submit. When you are with him forget everything that I taught you about the pleasures of sex. Be a rag doll and submit only with your body and not with your passion. Be so boring that he'll never repeat the assault.'

'What if I just explain to him that I'm not interested,' Pandora sounded desperate.

'Pandora, you must avoid denying Zeus, or having any arguments with him. Never say to him that he is wrong, even when he is. I've made this mistake once too often. You don't have to make it also.'

The three stiffened when they spotted Zeus walking up to them. He stopped as he drew near. He smiled and Pandora recovered sufficiently enough to be able to return his smile.

'Sorry to interrupt. This gathering will be ending soon and I'd like to present my gift to you.'

Both Hermès and Aphrodite performed an exaggerated bow as they turned to leave. As they walked away, Pandora was left standing with Zeus, both seemingly trying to out smile each other.

'I told everyone that I'd be the bearer of your final gift, Pandora,' he explained.

She smiled and stiffened at the same time.

'My gift is the gift of hope. Hope is a feeling of wanting something you desire to happen. When you experience a setback, you can always turn to hope to solicit a favourable outcome. Hope will give you strength to persist and persevere, even when the reality of the situation appears bleak.'

Pandora thought of the irony of his gift. 'Thank you, Zeus. I accept your amazing gift graciously and I already feel enriched for it.'

'Are you happy with today's events?' he queried.

'Yes, I'm ecstatic. I have established new friendships with wonderful people, and I've received many wonderful gifts from them. I would also like to use this time to thank you for my life, and for all the wonderful opportunities you have afforded me. I believe I must now submit my body to you, as some form of reward or payment.' She said it without trepidation or hesitation, and it sounded much like a commercial transaction where a remittance was now due for services rendered.

'Interesting, an offer I didn't anticipate.'

Pandora believed he was lying. She smiled and placed her hand on his chest and caressed it as she moved in closer to him. She whispered seductively, 'You are my king, lord, and my master, and therefore I am all yours to take for your amusement and bodily pleasures.'

Zeus grinned at her. He then instinctively looked over her shoulder only to confirm that Hera was intently monitoring their encounter. Her scowl caused him to grimace, but he managed to returned his attention to Pandora.

Pandora showed no sign of witnessing the silent communication between Zeus and his wife. She moved even nearer, the warmth of their bodies radiating onto each other. 'I'd make an excellent pupil to a god of your experience and legendary talents for mutual physical arousal.'

She moved her hands to feel his muscular arms and she groaned in an admiring rapture. She moistened her lips imperceptibly as she slowly moved her hips toward him, pressing the mounds of her breasts into his chest. The effect on Zeus was disarmingly predictable as his face portrayed the look of a frightened prey under the gaze of a determined predator.

Zeus smiled and he slowly drew away from her. 'Your offer is generous, but unnecessary. I have no plans to bed you. I desire for you to remain intact for your future husband.'

'Am I to be married off?' she asked flatly.

'Yes, but not to a human. You will remain here at Mount Olympus, married to one of us. You will submit to your husbands will,' he explained, paused and then continued. 'If you do so willingly, and prove that you are both pleasing and obedient to your husband, you will have a fulfilling life, and I will grant you immortality.'

Pandora said nothing.

***

By the time the party concluded, Pandora was left feeling both elated and confused. She was delighted to have been treated in this way. As far as she could tell, she was the first human to have ever been afforded such an honour. She had received an overwhelming amount of good advice on how to conduct her life. She now planned to put her writing skills to good use by documenting all that she had been taught. On top of all the verbal gifts bestowed upon her by the gods and goddesses, she also had many wonderful actual gifts. She was especially thrilled about the jewellery, even Aphrodite's expression upon seeing them confirmed their magnificence. It was a pity about Hera's harsh backlash. That woman might cause her trouble, and she'd have to somehow devise a strategy to neutralise any negative interference or pessimistic influences by her.

The one aspect that troubled Pandora the most was the pronouncement that she was to be given off in marriage to someone of Zeus' choosing. The prospect of marriage didn't bother her too much. Aphrodite taught her that men were easily satisfied and mostly manageable. If she decided to live the life of a party girl, despite being married, she would do so anyway. Zeus however, might choose a formidable, powerful, and controlling god to be her husband and that relationship might end up being bad for her.

Pandora decided that it was better to remain positive. Besides, her future husband might like to party also. A life of immortality was a life she was prepared to accept. She hoped that she would be able to party without too many consequences. It then occurred to her that it was Zeus that gifted hope to her. Pandora pondered this for some time and concluded that it was an omen. What she didn't know was if it was a good omen, or a bad one.

She returned to Aphrodite's home and found it to be devoid of activity. She briefly wondered where her host was, but decided that she needed to be alone to write all of this down so that she could rest comfortably, and hopefully sleep untroubled by all the events that had happened to her since Zephyrus breathed life into her.

Drawing from a stack of blank parchments, she dipped the writing quill into the ink pot and started by first writing down all the lessons she had learned from Hermès, including the extra one's he taught her today.

Her list from Hermès looked like this.

- *Hermès taught me that...*
- *There are two types of utterings. The first type is collaborative and the second type is commanding. Their main purpose is to get other people to do for me what I want them to do.*
- *Know how to always give praise.*
- *'Confidence is king, let it rule me.*
- *Show concern without actually feeling it, or even doing anything for them.*
- *Never raise my voice, especially in anger.*

- *Never admit to making a mistake, and never apologise if I do.*
- *Keep a record of everyone's else's mistakes, secrets, and weaknesses.*
- *Be contradictory about everything.*
- *Use rational argument to keep them unbalanced and off-side. Let them feel weak and confused, and make them believe that I am strong.*
- *If I don't have an answer, I'll be evasive. I'll deflect the conversation toward something I can control knowledgeably, and then I'll bedazzle them.*
- *If I ever feel that I must capitulate, then I'll make it seem like it was my idea to do so.*
- *Never accept payment of any sort. They must at all times remain indebted to me.*
- *Never share my secrets with anyone.*
- *Move all feelings of guilt away from me and on to them.*
- *If the relationship is becoming sour, or I feel I'm losing control or influence over another person, then I'll discard them.*
- *Other people are a resource, I'll keep them close, only whilst they have value.*
- *I'll be on the receiving end of life's riches, not the giving.*
- *Whatever is happening, I'll always smile sincerely.*
- *I'll use the word yes as often as I can. If my answer is no, then I'll stall before uttering it. I'll always delay the negative and reinforce the positive.*
- *I'll immediately repeat back the other person's name as if it was the sweetest name that I have ever heard.*
- *I'll only talk about the small mistakes that I have made, and I'll apologise sincerely for errors, so that others will become more willing to confide and trust in me.*
- *I always show genuine interest in everyone.*
- *I am a great listener.*

Pandora next wrote down the teachings she learned from Aphrodite.

· *Aphrodite taught me the art of being female.*
· *Uncompromising beauty is my valuable asset that I control.*
· *I will always secure benefits before giving my heart and body to another.*
· *I am desirable and therefore entitled to a great life.*
· *I'm always happy and grateful.*
· *I use grace, poise, and I'm the master of the art of sexually pleasuring a male.*
· *Never put myself at risk of getting pregnant.*
  (unless I want a child??)
· *Enjoy sex on my terms and for the pleasure it gives me.*
· *Dress in clothing that reveals much, but not everything.*
· *My sexiest feature is my voice. My words when combined with my body movements, will deliver to me any man into complete submission.*
· *I'll cleverly reveal my desires and explicit sexual fantasies with them, as it'll drive them deeper into my control.*
· *Males will do almost anything for me on the hint of reciprocated affections.*
· *Maintain cleanliness and hygiene at all times.*
· *Dress sexy and wear a modest amount of jewellery. Don't be flashy.*
· *Smell appealing at all times.*

Pandora next decided to write down the few bits of advice that Hebe shared with her.

· *Always give honest and sincere appreciation for everything that anyone does for me.*
· *Arouse in others their desire to become invested in my happiness.*
· *Let them believe that it was their idea to help me.*
· *Never complain about my life or criticise how others are treating me.*

· *Be upbeat and positive about everything all the time.*

Pandora also remembered that Zeus gave her some of his words of wisdom.

· *Emotions are often mirrored. If I seem happy toward someone, then they'll more likely behave happily towards me. If I'm angry, then they'll reflect that anger back at me. If I'm loving and kind, then they'll mirror my behaviour, and they'll be loving and kind in return.*
It is important to take the initiative and remain in control of your situation.
· *Caution. By being happy when someone is angry or upset with me can amplify their bad mood, not reverse it.*
· *But, if their anger is with someone else, then by being sympathetic, I will help calm them and make them an ally.*
· *If I am in a position to help someone with their problem and then by doing so, I'll increase their loyalty toward me, then I will help them.*
· *I'll become a respected and trusted problem solver, as this is a powerful quality to have.*

Next, she documented all the gifts she had received from the various gods and goddesses. She thought it'd be nice to use large lettering and a single parchment for each one as it felt more impressive.

Hephaestus - *writing quill (now in use)*

Athena - *The power to control my fears and to never feel despair.*

Hera - *The relief from exhaustion, and the strength and perseverance to carry on regardless of the enormity of the task.*

Persephone - *The power to accept my fate, and the realisation that I mustn't fear death, or be saddened by the prospect of dying.*

Demeter - *The freedom from the fear of being hungry.*
There will always be fruits, crops, and animals to harvest for their food. It shall be plentiful, tasty, and nutritious. I'll live my life knowing that I will always have good food on my table.

Plutus - *Enjoying my life with the freedom from poverty.*
The lands will always provide me with the means to have
enough of what I need or want.
Apollo - *The remedy of illness, and the treatment of injury.*
I'll live a healthy and safe life with the knowledge to cure all that
ails me, and the skills to repair my injuries.
Aglaia - *A brooch made of white rough-cut diamonds,*
and a mixture of emeralds and peridot gems, shaped like a
waterfall cascading out of a lush jungle.
Euphrosyne - *A wrist band made from blue sapphires and*
topaz gemstones,
with small yellow citrine stones and tiny amber stones, symbolising
where the ocean meets the sandy beach.
Thalia - *A necklace of emeralds, peridots, and rubies held together*
by strands of gold chain in the shape of a tree with smoky
brown quartz as the trunk and branches, symbolising the tree of life.

Pandora studied the three pieces of jewellery she had laid out on the table before her. She was pleased that she owned them, and she knew she would treasure them forever. She was also satisfied with herself about how she had accurately documented their appearance and significance. Smiling, she carefully wrapped each piece in quality cloth, the way Aphrodite had demonstrated when packing away her own magnificent jewellery.

She rolled each of the parchments separately, but couldn't find any string to hold them bound. She shrugged and fetched a large clay storage jar and firstly stowed her jewellery, followed by each of the rolled scrolls. She left out the quill as she thought it would remain in use as she continued to document her lessons and learnings. She put the lid on the jar. It was closed, but she felt it didn't offer her the security she desired for her precious booty. So, she next took some sheets of bee's wax and carefully moulded the wax over the lid. She lit a candle and using the flame, she carefully melted the wax over the lid, creating a tight seal.

When the task was completed, she blew out the candles flame, and closely examined the jar. She was satisfied that her valuables were now in an anonymous container, and that the lid was properly sealed to prevent moisture from getting in, or from insects entering and damaging the parchments. Pandora was totally satisfied that her treasures were safe. She sighed, feeling relaxed. She yawned, stretched and decided that now was the time to have some much-needed rest. She carefully hid her jar among the others on a sturdy timber shelf. Next, she disrobed, climbed naked into bed, and promptly fell into a deep sleep.

***

The following morning Hermès nudged her awake. Pandora grumbled a complaint as she rolled in her bed, slowly opening her eyes. She looked into Hermès face and smiled. 'This is a pleasant surprise. What are you doing here?'

'I was curious as to how you avoided being defiled by Zeus?' he asked calmly.

'I offered myself to him, as you hinted that I should, but he surprisingly declined. He said that it was better that I remained intact for my future husband.'

'Do you know what that means?' he was curious.

'Aphrodite explained it to me.'

'Good.'

'Zeus didn't tell me the name of the god I'm to marry. Do you know who he is?'

'I know it isn't me,' Hermès sighed.

Pandora sat up and hugged him. She felt his muscular body envelop hers and she turned her face so that her lips could find his, but he pulled away.

'I can't,' he cried.

'I know.' Pandora looked devastated. She knew she was in love with Hermès, despite Aphrodite having explained that her feelings were only as a result of his kindness and her gratitude toward him. The lessons of life that he had provided, and the closeness that they had shared from their time together, made it feel natural for her to fall in love with him. Aphrodite had also warned her to ignore these feelings that she had developed for Hermès, as they would cloud her mind and distract her from other more worthy associations and liaisons.

'Zeus came to visit me this morning. He told me that the god that you are to marry is presently working in the human village. He asked me to come here to tell you.' He paused. 'Perhaps, I could take you out there to find him.'

'Should I seek him out?'

'Only if you really want to. I don't know who he is, but you never know, he may be pleasant. If he is helpful to humans, he may be a kind hearted and a loving husband toward you. You might even find yourself being happy with him, and...' his voice trailed off.

'When I've washed, dressed, and eaten, I'll visit the human village and see if I can find him and learn a little about him.'

'Do you want me to come with you?' he offered.

'No, your presence will be a sure sign of who I am. I think I'd be better served if I mingle incognito.'

'True,' he paused considering. 'You can at least have a meal with me before you go off to discover your fate,' he invited.

Pandora realised she was hungry and happily nodded her acceptance. After her ablutions she dressed and found Hermès lounging in the garden. They found the cook and requested several fried eggs, crispy bacon rashers, oven baked bread, and freshly squeezed orange juice. They relaxed in the atrium waiting for their food as they talked about yesterday's reception and all the wonderful gifts she had received.

When the food arrived, they ate, drank, and laughed, both realising that this may be the last time that they could do this alone together. When Pandora became formally betrothed, it might become more difficult for the two of them to engage even in harmless social intercourse.

Hermès stood as if making to leave. Pandora whimpered so he leaned forward and gently kissed her lips. 'That may have been my last opportunity to do that,' he explained smiling as he drew back.

Pandora's eyes were still closed. 'Don't go,' she pleaded.

'Goodbye my star pupil.' He turned and left, walking hastily toward the exit and out of her life. Hermès had already decided that it was now a good time for him to visit his uncle Hades, and so took his leave from the frivolous activities of Mount Olympus. Hermès headed directly for the one place that accurately reflected his mood.

Pandora wept.

***

Later in the day, Pandora changed into sensible clothing and secure footwear for her visit to the human village. She added a shawl
and wore a silk head scarf. Next, she organised a water bottle that had
a secure strap that she arranged to carry comfortably over her shoulder and across her body. She now felt prepared for her journey and,
with some trepidation, she set off in the direction of the human village at a comfortable walking pace.

The stretch of land that separated the gods from the humans was
lightly wooded. The tall trees, many in bloom with a plethora of flowers, hummed with the sounds of bees and other insects. Pandora saw
many birds weaving through the air in pursuit of their insect prey.
The birds chattered, squeaked, and squawked happily, indifferent to
Pandora's encroachment. The sky was a vivid blue, and the sun basked
Pandora in its warmth. She muttered a polite appreciation to Helios,
the god of the sun.

The wind blew as a gentle breeze which cooled her as she walked.
She didn't know the direction it came from, so she didn't offer any
gratitude. She knew not to make the mistake of thanking the wrong
wind god, as their wrath, when offended, could be quite blustery.

Pandora had no appreciation of the trees and shrubs that she saw
on her journey. She saw some animals foraging, but neither recognised what type they were, or had any sense of curiosity or wonder-
ment about them. Flowering plants that would have delighted most
people, produced little interest for her. Even the freshness of the air
didn't register as a positive to her. Pandora was a relationships person,
and her whole life had been about engaging in associations in such a

way that they would benefit her. The natural world didn't register to her. Its bounty was promised, but the beauty of it was unappreciated and ignored.

Pandora thought about who she might meet. She knew that humans lived in the settlement that she was headed to. There, she would meet human males and she planned to engage them in conversation in order to learn more about them. She already had diminished expectations, as she was reliably informed that they were basic simple creatures. So, she had already concluded that she was well and truly above them, despite her being as much a human as they were. Zeus had explained to her that many human women had now also been created. She hoped that they were sufficiently progressed so that she could meet and assess them also. She already doubted her willingness to bond with any of them. Pandora decided that she was in the body of a human with the mindset of an eternal. Her main mission was to make the conversion from human mortality to become an immortal goddess. She planned to become a favoured goddess and live a long and ecstatic life. She was here to meet her future husband, as marrying him was her pathway to achieving all of her goals.

She slowed her pace as she neared a crude structure by the pathway. She recognised that it had walls and a roof. There was a door, but it was open, as were the holes that might have worked as windows. It was held together by reeds and fibres and didn't look either clean or safe. Entering the structure didn't appeal to her, and offensive odours emanated from its direction.

But Pandora was curious if anyone resided there. Standing about ten paces away from the opening, she called out. 'Hello, is there anyone inside?'

She heard mumblings and grumblings emanating from the room. Clearly, she had disturbed someone's slumber. A human male, wear-

ing only a loin cloth, stood in the door opening. He appeared dishevelled as if he'd just woken up. His skin was smudged in several places
with dirt, and he gave off an offensive body odour that was apparent
even from the distance that separated them. Pandora resisted a desperate urge to withdraw.

'I am Pandora,' she explained. It didn't register to the human. 'I'm
from the gods.'

The human yawned and then stretched. He scratched and rubbed
his abdomen. His hand reached up to his face and he was about to
pick his nose, but he hesitated as if remembering some recent rep-
rimand. He seemed totally disinterested in Pandora and stood firm,
staring blankly at her.

'What's going on out there?' a voice asked and its owner appeared
at the door standing next to the man. It was a human female. She
was wearing an off-white cloth body wrap which was loosely tied in
a knot, just above her breasts. She too looked dishevelled.

'I'm looking for the gods who work here with you?' Pandora explained.

They looked at each other as if hoping that they could find a response to what Pandora was saying. Neither spoke and they turned to
look at Pandora some more.

Pandora took their silence to mean that they needed more information, so she continued. 'They are working to help people, like you,
to build homes, plant crops, and raise farm animals. You must know
of them.'

'Do they look like you?' the woman asked.

'They are male gods. I don't know their names.'

'Prometheus and his brother are working by the river,' the man offered. He belched, sniffed, spat, and then scratched his nose. Neither action raised the ire of the woman who pulled hair away from her face, tucking it behind her ears. She was grinning excessively at Pandora, checking her clothing and admiring the confident way she presented herself.

'The river?'

The man pointed.

Pandora nodded her appreciation and headed in the direction that the man had indicated. She passed several more humans, all looking the same as the couple, modestly dressed and generally dirty. Pandora wondered that if there was a river close by, why didn't they use it to wash themselves and their clothing. She decided to share her feelings on the subject when she found the gods that she was seeking.

As Pandora continued walking down the path, the number of dwellings increased, but she was unimpressed with any of them as they all looked like hovels. Each of them had a blackened outdoor fire place which was surrounded by what could be used as chairs. They didn't look clean or comfortable, and so Pandora decided that she'd avoid using them.

Pandora also noted the prevalence of four footed, fur covered beasts that happily accompanied the humans. They looked friendly enough and they seemed at ease with the humans. Pandora decided she didn't want to know what they were or to talk to any of them. They looked hairy, motley, dirty, and exuded highly undesirable odours. From their constant panting and salivating, she assumed they'd have limited language skills. Then one of them barked several times and shifted its tail from side to side in a rapid motion, confirming her conclusion. The beast came nearer to Pandora and sniffed her legs making Pandora feel a little on edge.

She kept walking in the general direction that the first man had pointed to her, hoping it was towards the river. She assumed it was the right way, as the path was well worn, indicating multiple users which made sense as it was the path to get water, an essential for all life.

She heard the noise from the river before she saw it. The current was strong at this part of the river. Having never seen one before she found herself mesmerised by the flowing of water over rocks. The roar it made was oddly scary and reassuring at the same time. The width of the river was at least six times her own body length. She assumed that the speed of the water, and the rapid way it flowed over the rocks, that it would be dangerous to try to cross it. She was warned of the dangers of drowning when she first experienced bathing in a calm pool of warm water, prepared for the purpose of cleaning her body.

Pandora looked up and down the river, hoping she'd locate the two gods who were working with humans in some resource providing function. She didn't see either one, so she was startled when one of them pretended to shove her bodily into the water, but at the same time he held her back to prevent that from happening. She turned angrily to confront her trickster, but relaxed as she recognised him as a god that she had previously seen at her welcoming party. He had remained distant from her, so they had never met or talked, but she knew from hearing it from others, that he was a god of some significance.

She also remembered that he was one of the gods that didn't have a gift, or even any words of advice for her. She decided that she didn't care as he was tall, strikingly handsome, and sported a welcoming smile. She smiled happily in return.

'My name is Prometheus,' he explained.

'I'm Pandora.'

'Yes. I know who you are.'

'Do you know why I'm here?'

'You'd like to discover who your future husband is.'

'That's correct,' she agreed. She suddenly hoped that it would be him, as he seemed very nice. 'Is it you?'

'No.'

'Do you know who he is?'

'Yes, you are to marry my brother.'

'Is he like you?' She quickly decided that she'd learn as much as she could about him, whilst she had this opportunity.

'We're brothers,' he replied as if that explained everything. He drew in a deep breath. He had already decided that this woman wasn't suited to Epimetheus. She would make him miserable.

'What are you doing here?' she queried, looking at the channel that the men were digging. She had no knowledge about engineering and couldn't work out what she was seeing.

'We're constructing an aqueduct that I designed. We want to use the force of the rivers flow to divert some of its water down this channel. In that way it will fill a large reservoir of water which can be used by all when the river levels are too low in summer.'

Pandora found this topic boring, and so she changed the subject. 'Do you have a special skill or attribute, Prometheus? All gods seem to specialise or have some preference as to how they devote their energies.'

'Firstly, I am a titan, not a god. My most important role was the creation of humans, but I also designed many of the animals and some of the plants that you see about you.'

'But not me.' Pandora didn't care much about animals or plants.

'No. But I am responsible for creating all of the others. Now, I care for them. I am their teacher, champion, and their protector.'

'Do you spend a lot of your time with the humans, helping them?'

'I find myself preferring human company than that of the gods and goddesses of Mount Olympus,' Prometheus explained as he looked at Pandora, and then he added, 'You know, you do look out of place here away from the magnificent camaraderie of the immortals. Are you uncomfortable being out here and within the human's domain?'

She could tell that he wasn't being pleasant about the inhabitants of Mount Olympus. He spoke like that he held the other gods in some contempt. She speculated that it may be the leadership that he didn't like, as she had heard numerous rumblings from others about the uncomfortable discord that Zeus and Prometheus exhibited towards each other.

'What does your brother do?' she asked, steering the subject away from her being misplaced.

'He has created many of the animals and plants that we have today. He specialises in the fiddly bits ensuring infinite diversity. He does get chided by others for the range of differences he establishes, and the time and resources he spends on each project.'

'Your brother is skilled at creating plants and animals?' Pandora re-iterated, trying hard to mask her disappointment.

'Yes. He is excellent at it. Each plant and animal share the same basic structure, but he adds some distinguishing feature that makes it unique.'

'I've had nothing to do with animals. They look weird and dirty,' she concluded.

'They certainly don't have our need for cleanliness,' Prometheus agreed. 'But you'd be surprised about how many of them have grooming techniques.'

'Is your brother clean?' she was concerned.

Prometheus laughed. 'For the most part he is. Our work often renders us filthy, but he scrubs up well.'

'I look forward to meeting him.'

'I know. I'm also the god of forethought and foresight, so not much surprises me.'

'You knew that I was coming here, today?'

'Yes.'

'What's the difference?' she asked.

'Between forethought and foresight?'

'Yes.'

'Forethought is thinking about a project or an event before it happens. It allows for better preparation, perfected execution, and this often achieves optimum outcomes. Whereas, foresight is my ability to foresee and therefor prepare wisely for the future. I use logic and reasoning to make informed estimations of the outcomes for future situations. Both skills make me more strategic.'

'So, what other skills does your brother have. As I'm to become his wife, I suppose I should learn more about him.'

'His name is Epimetheus. Apart from his work on the creation of new life, he is also the god of afterthought and hindsight, which often makes him act too late for many things. For this reason, we often work together to balance each other out.'

'He sounds intriguing. Does being a god of afterthought and hindsight handicap him? I hope he doesn't get into too much difficulty.' Pandora was becoming a bit confused, and didn't appreciate the significance of her betrothed's role.

'Zeus has some exceptionally colourful expressions about him. He has never been married, but now that he knows about you, I can tell you that he is elated about becoming your husband.'

'That's a positive. I'm certain that a reluctant groom will develop into have a hopeless husband.'

Prometheus studied Pandora. She was exceedingly beautiful, a quality he knew that his brother would greatly enjoy. She was intelligent, and this would benefit Epimetheus enormously, provided she learned to appreciate him and love him unconditionally. She was a confident speaker, and this may make his brother shy and withdrawn, but she may also choose to use her skill to become the spokesperson for both of them. She could become his voice. She also seemed organised, and if this talent was channelled correctly, it would be a benefit to him, but if she directed away from the relationship, then it would tear them apart. Prometheus felt some trepidation about Pandoras impending marriage to Epimetheus, but he already knew that is brother was determined to wed her.'

'Why are you marrying my brother?' he asked. He sensed that he already knew the answer, but he wanted to hear it from Pandora.

'Zeus felt that it was the best outcome for me. I'm too much for a human male. They are weak and I am strong, and I'm destined for a much better life than what a silly human male can provide me.'

Prometheus conceded that her conclusion was accurate. 'But why my brother?'

'I don't know your brother, Prometheus.' She moved nearer toward him in a suggestive seductive manner. 'But if he is as good looking as you are, shares your intelligence, and has good intentions, then I'm confident that we can make it work,' she explained as if the whole process was a simple transaction. She studied his face and smiled and reached forward to rest the palm of her hand on his chest. 'Also, you and I could become enamoured,' she added with a mischievous twinkle in her eyes, and a slight suggestive parting of her lips.

Prometheus sadly concluded that Pandora's personality was one of sheer guile. She was shrewd, cunning, and she'd be quick to seize any opportunity by using her body, subterfuge, deceptions, and tricks to get what she wanted. He now felt incredibly sad and concerned for Epimetheus.

'What did Zeus promise you?' He had also felt like adding, "how did Zeus bribe you?" but he refrained.

'Immortality,' Pandora replied grinning, delighted with the prospect. 'My destiny is to live happily ever after,' she added proudly.

'I'm sure you are right.' Prometheus replied. To himself, he sounded unconvincing, but Pandora didn't pick up on it. She was twirling happily in a merry dance, and she was clearly delusional with the benefits of marriage and immortality. He knew several gods and goddesses who thought both were an unbearable burden.

Prometheus had long ago pondered the advantages of a marriage relationship. He concluded that a woman was ultimately bad for a man because she thinks independently and is therefore prone to having plots against him. Her conspiracy, is that she will have a different agenda to his, which is constantly clashing with his dreams and values. Or she'll have developed a poor opinion on how well he is managing their mutually agreed tasks, goals, and responsibilities. If a man avoids marriage and the difficulties it brings, he will be miserable in his old age because there will be no one to care for him, and his siblings will divide his property upon his death. However, as a married man with a good wife, he gets both the good and bad, but sadly he risks living his entire life in the everlasting agony of being criticised for always doing the wrong things, and according to his wife, constantly making poor judgments. Ironically, within the vast majority of couples, this aspect isn't seen as treachery, but simply accepted that this is just the way relationships are meant to be.

Prometheus had no plans to marry.

Pandora ceased her dancing when she picked up on Prometheus's sombre mood. If she was concerned for him, she didn't ask about the reason for it. 'Can you now take me to meet my betrothed?' she requested.

Prometheus nodded and they started walking down the hill toward a group of workmen who were excavating the soil to make the water reservoir. A tall, blond, clean shaven, handsome, semi-naked, male was clearly in-charge of the team of workers. Both his loincloth and body were muddied, as he and his team worked the layer of soft clay over the top of the compacted soil. The man-made water catchment was being lined to form a basin that would properly hold the water when it was diverted to it from the river. Prometheus called out to his brother. 'Epimetheus! There is someone special here to meet you.'

He looked up to see Prometheus standing next to the most beautiful woman he had ever laid eyes upon. He gasped audibly as he recognised her as being the woman of his hopes and dreams, and his future wife. The other men stopped their work and turned to see who their leader was looking at. They all grinned sheepishly realising that this must be the woman that Epimetheus had described to them when he informed them all that he was getting married.

Epimetheus struggled to extricate himself from the clingy clay. It made a watery squelching sound as he struggled to remain upright, as he fought against slipping as he slowly proceeded up the steep slope, closing the gap between them.

As he drew nearer, he extended his hand out toward Pandora in an act of welcoming friendship. As she offered her hand in response, he realised that his hand was filthy, so he quickly pulled it away and started to wipe it on his chest, but his chest was also dirty, so it did nothing to make his hand more presentable. He looked at it seemingly confused, but then quickly reached down to wipe his hand on his loin cloth, but it was also caked in clay, so he rubbed harder with the result that the bond holding his loin cloth to his body gave way, threatening to fall off him. He was immediately self-conscious, and using both hands he reached down to rescue the wayward cloth, but he stumbled and nearly fell backwards into the clay in the process. His balance continued to be compromised as his loin cloth slipped from his hands and flung into the air revealing his nakedness. He blushed in a vivid red in embarrassment as he scrambled after the cloth.

Pandora and the group of men, all burst into laughter. For Pandora, it was the most comical scene she had ever witnessed. Nudity was of no concern to her, and well, he was soon to be her husband and so she was sure she'd see him frequently naked in their future together.

Prometheus had merely grimaced. He knew first impressions we lasting, and he now feared that this scene was how she'd communicate to others about how well her first meeting with her future husband went.

'I'm sorry, Pandora. I should have realised that you were coming and I should have remained clean and presentable to meet you,' Epimetheus explained.

'I had intended to surprise you,' Pandora said laughing.

'Instead, it is I that have surprised you with a visual image that was perhaps more than you expected,' he added holding his cloth, barely covering his genitals. He offered her a boyish smile.

'Oh, I'm sure we'll get comfortably acquainted soon enough,' she said looking toward his groin.

Epimetheus shifted his weight uncomfortably.

'Perhaps you should wash in the river, and get properly dressed, and then you can continue your introductions in the more civilised setting of your home?' Prometheus suggested to his brother.

'Good idea,' Epimetheus agreed. He turned and headed for the river. As he crested the hill he stopped abruptly and turned. 'Sorry, I should have asked. 'Do you want to meet me at my home?'

Pandora smiled and nodded. Epimetheus' loin cloth hung limply from his left hand as he'd now dispensed with any attempt at modesty.

'Will you...?' he looked at his brother.

'Of course. Go!'

As Epimetheus disappeared over the ridge, Prometheus turned to Pandora. 'I'll escort you to Epimetheus house. I expect it'll become your new home.'

'I can't wait to see it,' Pandora agreed.

Prometheus had correctly surmised that Pandora anticipated a palace befitting the godly status that he and Epimetheus shared. But his home amongst the humans was little better than a human dwelling. They spend so little time at home that they did little towards grandeur, décor, or comforts. He could tell by Pandora's reaction that she was underwhelmed.

'Is this some type of titan humour that I'm unfamiliar with?' she asked cautiously. She turned to stare in disbelief at the inadequate structure some more.

'All it needs is a woman's touch,' Prometheus responded, trying hard not to make it sound like a joke.

'Not this woman.'

'Give it a chance.'

Epimetheus soon arrived. He was now clean and wearing a simple robe. Prometheus bade his farewell, choosing to leave the engaged couple to get to know each other. They watched his hasty retreat in silence.

Epimetheus motioned an invitation to go inside and so they entered the building. Security was lax and the door was unlocked. Humans respected their mentors and protected them. There was no concept of them entering uninvited.

Pandora surveyed the room, trying to imagine herself living here. The gods and goddesses knew how to live, but this place was meagre by her accustomed standards. Perhaps they'll be gifted better accommodation when they were married.

The furnishings looked crude and uncomfortable. The look of disappointment must have been apparent to Epimetheus as he hastily tidied some misplaced cushions on the chairs and Pandora witnessed dust waft into the air. I'm sorry, it now occurs to me that I should have tidied before your arrival. If I had, then this place might have made a better first impression.

Pandora tried to imagine the scope of enhancements required in order to improve her reaction to the dwelling. She desperately wanted to sound gracious to her future husband who was clearly happy to be sharing all his possessions with her, a total stranger. She tried desperately to form the words "It's lovely," in her mind, but quickly downgraded it to "It's quaint," before actually saying, 'Do you expect me to live here?'

'I suppose we could make some improvements,' responded Epimetheus who was puzzled by her reaction. His home was a mansion by human standard and quite adequate for his needs. 'What should we change?'

Pandora was tempted to say "All of it," but refrained drawing in a deep breath. She struggled with her teachings and now wanted to cry, or to be angry, or lash out a torrent of abuse about how did he expect her to be happy in a dump like this. She said nothing as she continued to scan the room. She looked at Epimetheus and then saw past him into another room. It looked like it might be a bedroom. She advanced, brushing past him, and entered the room. The centre piece was a large timber framed bed. It had a loose cloth covering a hay mattress, some cushions, and a blanket that looked like it hadn't been washed for some time. There was a long bench that had piles of unfolded clothes on it with just a tiny amount cleared for one person to sit. The window opening in the wall didn't even have a drape. She walked to the opening and stared outside. At least the view was impressive, looking down to the river, lush vegetation was in abundance and many of the trees were flowering. The area was nice, but the house was a dump.

She turned to Epimetheus. 'Is there a kitchen?'

'Yes, of course. You must be hungry and I should have offered you a beverage and some food. I don't have much, I suppose that in knowing that you were coming, I should have organised some refreshments and a meal, but I hadn't got there yet, being so busy with the construction of the water reservoir and all…'

'You knew I was coming?'

'Well, yes. Zeus visited me and told me that we were to be married, and well, you see, I explained that I really wasn't looking for a wife just yet, as I have my work, and you know that keeps me busy, and I gather from many, that wives are time consuming companion with their constant needs and demands and such.'

'When did Zeus visit? How long have you known that we were to be married?' Pandora demanded.

'It has been five passings by Helios,' he replied grinning.

'Five days…' Pandora murmured, deep in thought. Five days ago, she was still with Aphrodite. She was confused by all of this, as it was before the gathering when she was presented to the gods. 'Were you at my ceremony when I was being introduced to the gods and goddesses of Mount Olympus?'

'Yes, both my brother and I were there. You were very beautiful.' He paused to reflect as he looked deep into her eyes. 'I mean, you are very beautiful.'

'You were checking me out. Would you have agreed to marry me if I were ugly, or just plain?' Pandora was becoming angry. She felt frustrated about being manoeuvred as if she was some type of sociological experiment. She wasn't in control of the situation, or her life and wanted to better understand why she was being manipulated by Zeus in this way.

'Er, I guess so. I hadn't actually considered that I had any other option.'

'You were ordered to marry me?' Pandora was becoming upset. 'Was I your reward for services rendered? Some trade off for good measure?' How did you get to be in a position where you are told whom to marry.'

'Well...' Epimetheus started to explain the events of that day, but then hesitated and paused. The day was a bit confusing to him and perhaps they should be asking Prometheus as his memory was generally better than his. 'You see...' he uttered, stalling. He was silent for a moment but could tell that Pandora was becoming increasingly irate. 'Zeus...' he sighed. 'Zeus said that being married would make me into being a better god. He explained that I really needed a good, strong, and confident wife to manage me. He said you were the perfect person for that role. You could sort of take charge of our home and perhaps even speak for us...' his voice was trailing off again. Then he blurted, 'Prometheus isn't always there to help me, but as my wife, you'd be mine and we'd be together always.'

Pandora was crestfallen. She felt like she was some piece of waste to be discarded. She was now being forcibly tossed into the rubbish pile because that is where Zeus, and obviously Hera, had decided that was all she was worth. Was achieving immortality worth it. If she rejected this arrangement, could she ever find true love among the humans. Or, would she be able to transform this imbecilic titan into something that Mount Olympus society could respect. Was that her challenge? Is that why she was here?

'I'm to be your wife and you haven't even tried to hold me, or kiss me.' She was feeling worn out from her dilemma. She looked up at him and saw that he was leaning forward, eyes closed, and lips puckered up, as if now attempting to correct that oversight. He looked ridiculous, but she didn't laugh. Instead, she stepped back away from him. 'Not now,' she said as if chastising him. She was now also worried that she'd be doing that too often. She now studied him trying to imagine what sex with her future husband would be like. She grimaced and shuddered.

'I suppose you should know that I've never laid with a woman,' Epimetheus explained and he wasn't confident about announcing his inexperience. He had previously reasoned inwardly that his purity might have had some value to her, but now he was concerned that his virginity may be regarded as a negative. She may have hoped that she'd be marrying a strong, confident, experienced lover and he knew he wasn't adept at romance, or passion, or things physical like that.

'I had already figured that out for myself. Don't worry, I've been taught what to do, if and when it comes to doing that.'

'Should we try now?

'No!'

'Oh.'

'I'm going back home to prepare,' she explained to Epimetheus. She didn't elaborate on what she was preparing for.

'Where are you staying?'

'Aphrodite has given me a room to use while I sort out my future. She has been generous to me.'

'I don't really know Aphrodite that well, as we haven't spent any time together. Her skills and interests are very different to my own,' he explained. 'Is she a good friend?'

'I thought she was, but now I'm not so sure. She may have been in on this plan to...' she was about to add "set me up with you." But refrained, thinking that it would sound a bit cruel.

'It was nice meeting you, Epimetheus,' she said, unsure if it was true. She'd ponder his personality and decide if she could cope with being his wife. At least he was good looking, small compensation. Also, he was willing to be led by her, even though that might mean that she'd have to lead him through everything they did. She expelled a heavy sigh, and then without a word, exited the house.

She heard him call out. 'Good bye, Pandora.' She wondered why he didn't stop her or at least ask when they'd see each other again. She sighed and concluded that the question would occur to him long after she'd gone.

Pandora was sad and deeply conflicted. She wept silently as she walked slowly back to the comforts of Mount Olympus.

***

Her journey took her through the human village once more, and so she pulled her scarf over her head as if to disguise herself from the villagers. She shouldn't have tried as the fine, clean clothing she wore, clearly set her apart from the humans. Their dwellings, she couldn't see them as homes, were made from bunches of sticks held together with twine and mud. There were open fires which were used for heating pots with food cooking. She smelt their aromas in the air. They were neither appetising, nor unpleasant. Clearly their culinary skills had yet to be developed. The women appeared overworked, tired, and sad. Their introduction into human society was completed without ceremony or fuss, and most quickly paired off with the available men, quickly forming close bonds for protection and mutual affection.

The men seemed to have little purpose beyond agriculture and construction. They relied on the gods for inventions to improve their lives. Their role seemed to be there to worship and honour the gods and goddesses as Pandora saw numerous shrines erected in honour of them.

'We give you our thanks, dear lady, goddess,' a voice cried out behind her. Pandora turned and faced a slim young woman who was walking toward her. 'Your gift of life is appreciated by us all,' she added smiling.

Pandora looked into her vivid blue eyes. Most women had brown eyes, but hers were blue. For the first time it occurred to Pandora that variations in colour of hair, skin, eyes, height, weight, and facial features were as common with the humans as they were with the gods and goddesses.

'Will you be marrying Epimetheus and joining him in helping us?' the woman asked.

'I am betrothed to Epimetheus,' Pandora replied. It wasn't a commitment to assist, just a current status disclosure.

'You'd be most welcome,' the woman grinned some more. 'We need a woman's influence as Epimetheus and his brothers only think of practical things to teach us, but we know nothing of love or the pleasures of sex. There is no passion in our men. They think sex is sticking it into us, jerking it about, and then walking off after they have spilled their seed.'

'I assume they have seen animals copulate, and have learned from their example.' Pandora offered as a reason for the basis of human male copulation technique.

'Could you help us to teach them how to do it better?' the woman asked.

'How do you know that there is pleasure to experience?' Pandora was curious as to what inspired her request.

'Some of our women work at Mount Olympus. They have eyes and ears and know that goddesses are well pleasured by their males. We want that for us. Will you help?'

Pandora weighed up the responsibility. It felt like a heavy burden.

'Let me complete my marriage ceremony and after, when I'm settled, I'll tend to this for the sake of all human women,' she offered, not lying, but also not knowing if it would become true.

The woman hugged her. 'We'd be so grateful.'

Pandora broke free from the embrace. She smiled and nodded at the woman, turned and hastily continued through the village. Many of the woman came out to wave and smile gratefully at her. News obviously spread quickly here. Pandora now added the future of human female sexuality to her list of ponderings.

'May I walk with you?' a voice asked from the side.

She turned to see Prometheus walking toward her. She stopped and faced him.

'I'm heading to Mount Olympus and I thought if we journeyed together, we could talk about my brother,' suggested Prometheus.

Pandora nodded. Some more information and insight into Epimetheus character would be of significant value to her at this point. They both turned to the direction of Mount Olympus and started a brisk walk.

'My brother means well. His heart and his intentions are always good,' Prometheus explained.

'Yet, he comes across as thoughtless,' Pandora replied sounding harsher than she intended.

'He can't help it. That is his role in our universe. I'm the god of forethought and he is the god of afterthought. We are brothers and we had represented these conditions from birth. We'll never change as this is our destiny. We work closely together so we can minimise the negative consequences of his condition.'

'Is there no remedy?' Pandora was hopeful.

'None, only his death will release him.'

'But he is immortal.'

Prometheus nodded. She was beginning to comprehend.

'My brother and I serve as examples of future behaviour. My role is to be a role model of what to do more off. I serve as a guide to leading a better life through preparedness, equipping them for the tasks and challenges that they'll confront. They learn the benefits of being more like me and they reap the rewards.' He paused, but she didn't say anything. 'I teach them to save seeds for future crop plantings, building strong weather proof shelters so that they'll have protection from the harshness of winter, gathering wood to burn and storing it in a dry place so that they'll have fire for heating and cooking, when the forests are wet from the winter rains.'

'I understand,' Pandora acknowledged.

'Epi, on the other hand serves as an example of the problems asso-ciated with not being prepared. He is the reason why we take a retro-spective examination of what we should have done better to improve the outcome. He is what we call learning from a bad experience. He is the reason we continue despite having setbacks. His role is vital as no-one, not even the gods, get it right the first time. Epi gives us strength, so that despite our lack of preparedness, despite all the mistakes we make, we continue to learn how to do it better the next time. Without Epi, many of us would be doomed to continually repeat our mistakes, never learning from them. His role is essential for the advancement of the human race.'

Pandora stopped walking and she looked at Prometheus who stopped next to her. 'Yet, he himself can never change. He'll never improve through his own lack of preparedness.' Pandora now better understood her fiancés' condition. 'He can't change or otherwise im-provements in the human condition would cease to happen.'

'You are a charming and an intelligent woman, Pandora. You might just be perfect for Epi, but only if you really wanted to be with him. Don't try to change him, just love him and manage him, support and comfort him. We need him to continue his vital role.'

'I'll think about it,' she said as a reply, stalling any offence. Pandora was thinking about the prospect from a 'What's in it for me," perspec-tive. She wasn't yet convinced that there was enough of it to progress this arrangement.

'I confess that I had originally warned Epi not to accept Zeus' offer of you as his bride. Any gift from Zeus always comes with a heavy price, most of which only becomes evident after the fact. I now feel that I was wrong about you, something that doesn't happen to me very often,' he said and grinned.

Pandora wasn't yet convinced that she wanted the life of being married to Epimetheus as her own. She wanted fun, sexual adventures, and a beautiful palace to call home. She wanted servants and cooks to clean for her, and tasty foods to be available whenever she hungered for them. She aspired to be more like Aphrodite, a strong, confident empowered female, and to live the life of abundance, fun and pleasures. Yet, Prometheus explained to her of a future life of humble service to a god and the humans he assisted. One whose main role was to be an example to others of what not to do. Her mental scales were tipping far away from this prospect.

They had now arrived at the gates of the walled city of Mount Olympus. The gates were unguarded, as there were never any threats to the city's inhabitants. The wall served its purpose as a delineation of the cities boundary's.

'Thank you for escorting me here, Prometheus. I appreciate the candid manner of your explanation and I have much to consider.' She looked into his face and then on impulse reached forward and kissed him on the cheek. She turned and headed for Aphrodite's palace.

Pandora walked into the building to find it devoid of activity. She was grateful that Aphrodite was out, probably partying with Ares performing all sorts of carnal activities. She decided to focus on her own issues. She found some food to eat. She sat in the garden pondering immortality as Epimetheus wife. Being a wife of a human male wasn't an option. Finding another god to marry would be prevented by Zeus. She only had the one option, but it didn't mean she had to like it. Later, when it was dark, she undressed, washed, and climbed into bed, only to have a restless sleep.

***

The following morning, Pandora awoke, dressed, and entered the living areas of Aphrodite's palace only to realise that she was still alone in the building. As much as she wanted to spend time with Aphrodite, and tell her of all that had happened, she was actually grateful that the titan goddess of love and sexuality wasn't at home. She had now reached her decision and worried that by telling someone else she may become clouded with alternative opinions, or even worse dissuaded from her resolve.

Pandora found some food, drank, toileted, washed, selected one of Aphrodite's power dresses to wear, donned firm footwear, took a deep breath, and left the property and set off to confront Zeus.

When she arrived, she was immediately escorted to his offices, almost as if they had anticipated her being there. She realised that she shouldn't have been surprised by this as Zeus was often several moves ahead of everyone else when it came to matters of importance within his domain.

'Pandora, welcome,' he said as she entered the room. He gestured to a chair opposite to his main office chair and invited her to be seated. She saw a jug of water and a drinking cup. She assumed these were placed there for her benefit, but it may have also have been there for some time. She suddenly imagined being poisoned by Zeus as a method of dealing with misfits, but she quickly dismissed that concern, as Zeus had numerous more demonstrative ways in which to deal with individuals that displeased him.

'Are you here to discuss your wedding plans?' he asked sweetly.

'Not quite.'

Zeus tried again. 'Are you here to discuss your preference to not marry, Epimetheus?'

'I am.'

'That's a pity,' concluded Zeus. 'Epimetheus was so delighted when I bestowed upon him a life companion such as yourself. He was very happy, and fully enthusiastic to be married to you and has started planning the ceremony.'

'You and I both know that that is not true,' Pandora sighed. 'He is incapable of preparing anything until after the event is concluded.'

'I'm sure that isn't true,' Zeus chided.

'It's mostly true,' Pandora corrected. 'It is his main purpose. He is among us to serve as a lesson on how to improve ourselves, to make mistakes and learn from them. He is hindsight and cannot, and will never change. He is needed exactly as he is.'

'But he does deserve a loving and devoted wife.'

'That is probably true, but it doesn't have to be me. He'd be far happier with someone who wants him as he is. Someone who can love him unconditionally, someone who can enjoy a happy life knowing that her husband meant well, but couldn't organise a party in an ale house.'

Zeus appreciated the quality of the insult.

'I am disinclined to agree to this marriage. I do not want this as my fate. I plan to marry out of love, friendship, and mutual respect, and I believe that I will never respect Epimetheus.'

'Pity, I have a wonderful gift planned for you.'

'Immortality.'

'Yes, there is that. You must marry a god to achieve it. Any old god would do, but you must understand this. No-one, other than Epimetheus, will have you as their wife.'

Pandora considered the implications of what she was hearing. Zeus had just confirmed her belief that he had warned all other potential suitors, especially Hermès, away. If she was fated by Zeus to marry Epimetheus or live a mortal life then so be it.

'You mentioned another gift?

'My father's planet has several moons that need to be named. I shall name one Pandora in your honour and whenever anyone examines the night sky, they'll be reminded of your place among the gods and goddesses of Mount Olympus. I have selected one for your intended, as well as his brother.'

'I thought you didn't like them?' sneered Pandora.

'I don't especially. They both served me well during the Titanomachy, but they have been a great discomfort to me ever since. They are titan's you know.

'I know.'

'History has it that Prometheus knew that their titanic struggle was doomed to lose, so he convinced his brother for both of them to fight on your side.'

'We Olympian's prevailed,' Zeus agreed. 'And, we have ruled ever since.'

'Why have humans at all?' Pandora demanded.

'To be worshiped by our humans is our single source of power. We are immortal through them. We nurture them, and encourage them to expand their numbers so that they can better revere us.'

'So, when I become immortal, I too will become dependent on their love for me for my existence?'

'I always said you were a clever girl, Pandora. You continue to impress me.'

Pandora gave off a half smile. She examined the god king. He looked smug. 'If I refuse to marry Epi,' she paused, 'Epimetheus, what will be my fate?'

'You will be banished from Mount Olympus and everyone here will alienate you. I might add that this outcome is heavily supported by my wife, Hera.' Zeus paused. 'You will end up being an emotional plague on all humans, as you will be seen by all to be a disappointment and a disgrace, having wasted the opportunity to do so much good for them.'

Pandora said nothing.

'Would you like some more time to ponder your decision?' Zeus asked kindly.

'Yes,' Pandora replied. She stood up, turned, and hastily departed from his office. By the time she was at the palace exit, she was weeping inconsolably.

***

When Pandora returned to Aphrodite's home, she saw that the goddess had returned. She was sound asleep, so Pandora maintained her silence so as to not awaken her. She slipped off the dress and walked naked into Aphrodite's bed chamber, and returned the borrowed dress to its correct place. Carefully, she walked out of the room, through the palace, and into her own room. She next selected a simple day dress and slipped it on. Looking about the room she spotted her jar of valuables. Owning them gave her great comfort, so she took the jar off the wooden shelf and hugged it. She looked through the window opening and realized it was a lovely day. She decided to sit in the warmth of the sunlight and review her discussion with Zeus. She started crying again. Carrying the jar, she sat outside on a bench overlooking the garden beds, the flowering plants lifted her spirits briefly, as she pondered her options.

'Pandora, are you here?' Aphrodite's voice boomed through the open window. Pandora didn't want Aphrodite to see her storage jar. She set it down, arose, and entered the room.

'There you are,' Aphrodite greeted her. 'What were you doing outside?'

'Thinking.'

Aphrodite looked outside to figure out the attraction. The sunlight hurt her eyes and she shook her head dismissively. 'It's too bright for me out there. Let's find a darker place to sit and talk. I had a heavy night of drinking and all this sunshine is bad for me.'

Pandora followed Aphrodite into the day room. She pulled the curtains closed and the room became darker. They selected comfortable couches to lay down on and Aphrodite slowly described the events of her previous evening.

'Ares was insatiable last night. I tell you I've never had so much sex in one evening.' Aphrodite winced as if in some discomfort. Even getting him blind drunk didn't slow him down,' she laughed. 'Naturally, I had to match him drink for drink, and orgasm for orgasm. That boy sure is competitive.'

Pandora felt that she couldn't contribute to the conversation. She suddenly thought of Hephaestus. He and Aphrodite were briefly married. He was such a kind god, but a definite mismatch for Aphrodite. She wondered what he'd think of his former wife's current behaviour.

'So dearest. How was your meeting with Epimetheus?'

Pandora spent the next hour telling Aphrodite all about her trip to the human village, her talks with Prometheus and her fateful meeting with Epimetheus.

Aphrodite was a good listener and barely interrupted her monologue of events, fears, worries, and unbalanced options. When Pandora seemed to have finished, she offered her one and only conclusion. 'You my dear, are in a tragic situation.'

'What should I do?'

'Do! Well, you only have one option. You must marry Epimetheus, and you must be a supportive and loving wife toward him. And you must help him with the humans, or you'll be doomed to remaining one of them.' She shook her head dismissively. 'You will be destitute, alienated, despised, and sorrowful. Your only pathway to immortality is to marry a god and the only god that'll have you is Epimetheus. After you're settled, you can have some fun as a party girl. There is plenty of room at Ares palace. You already know Thalia and the others. We always say "The more the merrier.'"

Aphrodite had it all worked out. She should fulfill her marital obligations, and then she could cheat on her husband. She could party like there was no tomorrow, because when your immortal, there are few consequences. Pandora was miserable. Her anger swelled and she ran from the day room. She entered her own bedroom and went outside intending to scream. She saw her jar and kicked it savagely. Her gifts were not treasures; they were the binding that entrapped her.

Whilst she was inside pouring her heart out to Aphrodite, Helios, the sun god, had weakened the beeswax seal of the jar holding secure the contents, all the gifts bestowed to her by her tutors, the gods, and goddesses of Mount Olympus. Pandora's powerful kick on the side of the jar tipped it onto its side, the lid flew off spilling out its contents, just as the four winds tussled for superiority. The mini twister lifted the paper scrolls out of the opened jar and drew them upwards in a powerful updraft. Pandora shrieked in panic, but the scrolls continued to rise. Then as suddenly as it all began, the winds calmed, the scrolls fell toward the ground some distance away. Pandora rushed to secure them, but all but one had fallen into a feature garden pond, the ink washing away from the paper as Pandora desperately reached into the water to retrieve them. Only one scroll escaped its watery demise. Pandora opened it and saw that it was the gift from Zeus. "When all else fails, hope will be all that remains." She pondered the irony of this new development. She couldn't help but feel that fate was manoeuvring her closer toward her marriage to Epimetheus.

She carried the gift of Hope back to the jar, checked the other items, especially that her jewellery was safe and secure, resealed the lid with new bee's wax, and placed it on the wooden shelf. As she pondered her loss, she thought that in hindsight it was irresponsible of her to leave the jar in the open air under the gaze of Helios. Even without being there, her betrothed was teaching her a valuable enlightenment.

The majority of her gifts were now just memories. She felt she could write them out once more, but the lessons taught to her by Hermès and Aphrodite were now losing their appeal, and she decided that she wouldn't need them. She began to accept that her path was a different one to the one that they had planned for her. She would marry Epi and she decided that she'd strive to be a loving, faithful wife, and respected partner to him.

***

The wedding of Epimetheus and Pandora was a simple rural wedding. Only Athena and Hephaestus attended from Mount Olympus, although Heph was positive he saw his father, perched high in a tree disguised in his eagle form, observing the proceedings.

There were many humans in attendance and they were delighted that one of their favourite gods had found and married such a delightful person. Pandora was quickly accepted into the human world. Her immortality, along with Epi's made them a long-term partnership instructing and assisting humans to become a strong and masterful race of beings. Women everywhere were taught how to nurture their menfolk into being loving, responsible husbands. Pregnancies abounded, and they were all very happy worshiping the gods and goddess who continued to watch over them and guide them.

Pandora's importance lies cemented in mythology as she allowed for the procreation of the human race. As the first human woman, she was able to be the role model for all other women. She shared her gifts and knowledge, though somewhat diluted, with everyone. To this day, all humans believe, despite incredible adversity, that hope always remains.

Pandora and Epimetheus both enjoyed their marriage, and she quickly learned to love him and look out for his interests. His lack of forethought was often turned into a source of merriment and they were able to laugh off most of his shortcomings. Pandora had now fully understood and accepted his important role in society and its development and evolution. They had one daughter they name Pyrrha who was born with bright red hair.

Prometheus eventually married a goddess named Clymene, and together they had a son they named Deucalion. Their two children were dear friends and they eventually married.

During the one time when Pandora had the opportunity to speak publicly, she gave a memorable speech about her husband's role. Two sentences were particularly significant. "It is due to Epimetheus, that all of us have the capacity to accept that it is inevitable that we'll make mistakes. We know that it is okay to make mistakes, as long as we learn from them, and are prepared to honestly deal with any of the consequences." Her words resonated with the gods and the humans alike, and respect for Epimetheus continued to grow over time.

Pandora had a secret plain wooden box hidden in the darkness under her bed. It was without locking mechanisms and covered in dust, so as not to attract curiosity from others. From time to time, when she was confident that she wouldn't be disturbed, she'd drag the box into the light and open it. Inside, laying on a bed of wadding, was the original jar that she used to store her jewellery and messages. She would secretly open her jar, marvel at the jewellery, and re-read the one remaining message of hope. It was a reminder of her exciting, yet terribly misguided first days of life as a woman. She'd smile and think about how lucky that she wasn't that person.

Sometime later, well after the introduction of the first bulls and cows, Prometheus disappeared. It was presumed he was exiled for defying Zeus by gifting fire and teaching the humans how to cook meat.

It was an eternity before any of his family saw him again.

***

Footnote:

Pandora, Prometheus, and Epimetheus are all honoured astronomically as named moons of Saturn. Saturn is the Latin name for Cronus, father of Zeus. The gravity of the moons Pandora and Prometheus keep Saturn's rings in alignment, one orbits above the rings and the other below.

Novella one - Pisces

Novella one - the constellation Pisces and the story of Aphrodite and Eros, the Two Fishes.

Aphrodite is well known as the Greek goddess of love, romance, and sexuality. Aphrodite is also known to us as Venus, and the planet is named after her in her honour. This is the story of how Aphrodite came to be. Born in the ocean during a struggle between father and son, she was raised on an island. As an adult she was carried by Zeus to Mount Olympus to work and play with the gods and goddesses who lived there.

After a brief marriage to Hephaestus, she formed a steamy relationship with Hephaestus's brother, Ares and they had a son they named Eros. All her life, she struggled with the unwanted, yet amorous advances of the Titan monster named, Typhon. Eventually, she and Eros had to flee Mount Olympus to escape his wrath, and they eventually became the constellation of the Two Fishes known to us as *Pisces*.

Novella two - Capricorn

Novella two – the constellation of Capricorn and the story of Pricus the Sea-Goat.

Pricus is an old sea-goat with a problem. He is regarded as the old man of the sea. The younger generation wants desperately to abandon the old ways and leave their ocean home to live a more adventurous life on the land. The sea-goats are able to morph from sea-goats into land goats when they emerge from the surf to walk on land. They quickly learn to morph into human form, and to their delight discover that they can have much more fun exploring the plethora of opportunities that await them. In their naivety they make many mistakes, some ending in tragedy. Pricus is desperate to save the younger generation from themselves, and so must become increasingly resourceful do so, and do so in a way that his solution remains permanent. His dedication to his own kind earns him his place as the constellation of the sea-goat, known to us as Capricornus or *Capricorn*.

Novella three - Pandora

Novella three - Saturn's moon Pandora and the story of the first human woman.

Zeus, king of the Greek God's, commissions his son Hephaestus to craft the first human woman. Aided by Athena, he carefully researched the perfect form and then moulded her from clay He then painted and glazed her into the perfect woman. After being fired in his kiln, she was given the breath of life by the wind god Zephyr. She was named Pandora, being the bearer of the gifts bequeathed to her by the gods and goddesses of Mount Olympus. Her main purpose for humanity was to become the role model for all future human women. Zeus then commanded that she be properly trained so that she can navigate life's complexities, but her tutors do too good a job with her, and she becomes too powerful for a normal human life. Zeus became disillusioned with her, and he decided that she should be married off to a minor god, so that she'll do no harm to herself, or to others.

Pandora's story is so significant that she is honoured as *Pandora*, one of Saturn's moons.

Novella four - Taurus

Novella four - the constellation Taurus. This is the story of the Europa's meeting with Zeus as the white bull.

When Zeus, king and master of the gods and goddesses of Mount Olympus finds himself between wives he sets out on a desperate search for the perfect woman to marry. On a sunny field, set amongst spring flowers, on a stretch of land adjacent to the sea, he finds her. She is Europa, a gorgeous African princess. For Zeus, it becomes love at first sight. In his infatuation for this woman, he tries numerous times to impress her, and almost succeeds. Unfortunately for Zeus, his one true love is betrothed to another, and sadly for Zeus, a daughter must do her duty. Disguised as a magnificent white bull, he tries one last desperate attempt to win her affections.

The consequences of his quest for true love are celebrated as the constellation of the white bull, know to us as the ***Taurus***.

Also commemorated in this story is the constellation ***Draco,*** known as Ladon the Dragon. Also featured is Laelaps as the constellation ***Canis Major*** or Greater Dog, and the Teumessian Fox as the constellation ***Canis Minor*** or Lesser Dog.

Novella five - Scorpio

Novella five - the constellations Scorpio and Orion and the story of the scorpion verses the hunter.

Artemis is the goddess of the forests and of the hunt. She befriends a hunter named Orion. Their friendship is slowly progressing toward a blossoming romance when Orion boasts of his ability to wantonly kill all the animals that cross his path. Artemis is dismayed. Her policy is to only kill for food, to kill for pleasure is an outrage. She feels she must sacrifice her future relationship by stopping Orion from completing his boast. She manifests a giant scorpion and sends it to attack and destroy Orion. A massive battle ensues, and both are defeated, thus preserving animal life from indiscriminate killings.

To celebrate the outcome and to remind us that all life is precious, their images were cast into the heavens as the constellation *Orion* and the constellation of the Scorpion known to us as *Scorpio*.

Novella six - Aries

Novella six - the constellation Aries and the story of Chrysoma-llos the Ram.

Born from a union between Poseidon and Theophane on a remote island that was the home of a flock of sheep. They are interrupted by shepherds during copulation, so they disguised themselves as sheep to avoid the embarrassment that Theophane might suffer if their tryst became public knowledge. Their male child was born with the ability to morph from a human into a ram. From his mother, he has long golden hair, and when he becomes a ram, he has golden fleece. He has wings and the ability to fly.

He is named Chrysomallos and is raised by his loving mother Theophane. He eventually befriends the princess Helle, who lives in a nearby kingdom. When their lives become perilous, Chrysomallos the flying, golden fleeced, ram comes to her rescue.

His bravery is celebrated as the constellation of the Ram, know to us as *Aries*.

Novella seven - Ophiuchus

Novella seven - the constellation of Ophiuchus and the story of Asclepius the serpentius or serpent bearer.

Asclepius was the son of Apollo. When Apollo had to rescue Asclepius from his dying mother's womb, he realised that he did not know enough about medicine and surgery, and so he set about discovering as much as he could. He later taught all that he learned to his son. Next, to further his education, Apollo decided that Asclepius would learn even more from the tutor Chiron. Through him he completed his training and went on to be the foremost authority on how to manage illness and repair injuries. His wife Epione and he had five daughters and three sons, and all became involved in the practice of medical treatments. The most prominent daughter was Hygieia and the practice of hygiene is named after her.

Both Apollo and Asclepius have been forever revered as the fathers of medical treatments and their names were included in the original Hippocratic Oath, that all medical practitioners swore upon when becoming formally registered to become doctors.

His dedication to healing the sick and injured was commemorated in the night sky as the constellation *Ophiuchus*. Many people who practice in astrology believe that Ophiuchus is the unrecognised thirteenth star sign.

Also featured is the constellation of **Serpens** or "The Snake." Who Asclepius witnessed bringing healing herbs to another snake who was sick, and this event started him on his discovery of benefits of medicinal herbs.

Novella eight - Cancer & Leo

Novella eight - the constellations of Cancer and Leo and the stories of Karkinos the giant crab, Zosma the Nemean lioness, Astron the hydra, Aquila the eagle, Sagitta the arrow, and the constellation named after Herakles the Demi-God.

The birth of Herakles was surrounded by controversy. Being the demi-god son of the King of all the gods, he found it difficult to live a routine life with his wife and children.

Herakles was persecuted by Hera for being her husband Zeus's illegitimate son, and so he was inflicted by incessant painful headaches. He was told of a remedy by the oracle in Delphi, but before he could be cured, it required him to agree to take on many incredible tasks which were assigned to him by the local king. By completing these labours, he should be able to go on to live a long and fulfilling life.

He later became immortal, and Herakles is forever remembered as a Greek Mythological hero for defeating the giant crab that became known as **constellation Cancer**. He also killed the man-eating lioness that became known as the **constellation Leo**. He then slew the serpent of Lake Lerna, which is now known as the **constellation Hydra**.

Herakles used an arrow now known as the **constellation Sagitta,** to kill a giant eagle that became to be known as the **constellation Aquila** or "**The Eagle**".

Herakles was finally accepted at Mount Olympus and was honoured with the **constellation Herakles** also known as **Hercules.**

Novella nine - Gemini

Novella nine - the constellation Gemini and the story of the twins, Castor and Polydeuces.

Leucippe was desperate to become a grandmother. Fed up with her son-in-law's lack of progress, she asked Zeus for his assistance. When Zeus arrived, he took the opportunity, and disguised himself as a swan, and then he did much more than just arrange for Leda to become pregnant.

The Spartan twins grew up to become skilled horsemen, hunters, warriors, and adventurers. They embarked on many journeys together and their adventures included sailing on the Argo with Jason on his quest for the golden fleece, being hunters at the Calydonian wild boar hunt, and fighting Trojans at Troy. It was their sister Helen, who was the central reason for that protracted war.

The twins were honoured by Zeus for their bravery and commitment to each other, and he cast their image into the night sky to be forever remembered as the **constellation of the Twins**, which is now known as *Gemini*. Also featured in this story is the **constellation The Swan or *Cygnus*** .

Novella ten - Virgo & Libra

Novella ten - the constellations of Virgo and Libra and the story of the Astraea the maiden, and Themis the scales.

Astraea and Themis were both goddesses who were committed to advancing the living conditions of the humans who lived on the island of Thera. Along with other gods and goddess they believed that they would become the role models for all future human progress advancements.

However, the speed of their progress and their intentions to achieve self-determination worried Zeus. After inspecting the work and assessing all that had been achieved, he concluded that it must come to an abrupt end. And as every Greek immortal knows, when Zeus is determined and has made up his mind, nothing stops it his decision from happening. For Astraea the decision was devastating, so she cast herself into the night sky as "the maiden", forever watching in judgement over humanity as the **constellation *Virgo.***

Themis was later honoured for her balanced outlook on life, and is remembered as the scales as she evenly balanced out her reasoning and decisions. She is now known to us as the **constellation *Libra.***

Novella eleven - Aquarius

Novella eleven – the constellation Aquarius and the story of Ganymede the water bearer.

Ganymede was adopted by a family of shepherds when he was found abandoned as a young child. He preferred his own company, and whilst good at caring for the sheep he was regarded as a misfit by his adopted family.

One day, as he is tending the sheep, he was spotted by Zeus, who flying past in his eagle form. Out of curiosity Zeus landed to meet the young man and became quickly enamoured with him. Ganymede found himself attracted to the powerful God and very much wanted to be with him. Zeus easily convinced the young man to give up his shepherding life and come with him to Mount Olympus.

Ganymede became Zeus's friend and lover. He took over the role of cup bearer during important civil functions from Zeus's daughter Hebe, as she had found love and married a Greek Hero. Ganymede quickly became fascinated with aqueducts and fountains, and he was responsible for improving the water quality and availability of clean drinking water to Mount   Olympus's inhabitants. His contribution is celebrated as the **constellation of the "water bearer"** now know to us as the **constellation Aquarius.**

Novella twelve - Sagittarius

Novella twelve – the constellation of Sagittarius and the story of the "Archer" Crotus.

A water Naiad nymph named Eupheme was a demi-goddess of the Hippocrene freshwater spring near Mount Helicon. She was youthful, very beautiful, and powerful. She met and had a relationship with the God Pan, a Satyr, famous for playing the pipes was the god of shepherds, flocks, rustic musicians, and improvisation. Their romance led to the birth of Crotus.

Crotus was a Satyr and grew up to be like his like his father, preferring the company of muses. Most Satyrs preferred the company of Dionysus, God of wine, revelry, and debauchery, so Crotus was unusual in this way.

The muses were providers of inspiration to artists, musicians, poets, story tellers, artisans, entertainers, and dancers. They brought out the natural talents of those they inspired, and positively encouraged them to excel by pursuing their passions and striving for perfection in their chosen art form.

Crotus was also a great hunter, and many say that he invented the hunting bow. He was more popular as a musician and his most noteworthy contribution to   performance music was the addition of rhythmic beats used to accompany the musician's musical score. He was also responsible for the introduction of a   ritual applause to signify both pleasure from the performance and gratitude to the artist for their dedication to the composition and the quality of the performance. The applause was widely recognised as a significant motivator for artistic excellence.

Crotus was a mortal, and when he died, the Younger Muses petitioned Zeus to have his likeness immortalised as place in the night sky. Their petition was positively received, and, in his honour, he created the **constellation of the Archer** which is known to us as the **constellation Sagittarius.**

Novella thirteen - Centaurus

Novella thirteen – the constellation Centaurus and the   story of the tutor Cheiron.

Cheiron was a centaur who became the tutor to many of the legendary heroes of Greek mythology. Unlike other centaurs, Cheiron was intelligent, civilised and very kind. He was the teacher of students that included Jason, Castor, Polydeuces, Asclepius, Peleus, and Achilles and he taught them philosophy, archery, hunting, medicine, music, gymnastics, and the art of prophecy.

His life ended tragically when he was accidentally struck with a poisoned arrow by his close friend, Herakles. Herakles had loosed the arrow in an attempt to ward off marauding cruel centaurs who came to cause mischief to Cheiron, but in the confusion, Cheiron stepped into the path of the arrow and was stuck. His immortality prevented his death, but the strong   poison caused him everlasting agony. He decided to surrender his immortality to Zeus, so that he could pass into the underworld.

He was then commemorated as the **constellation of the Centaur** and is known to us as the **constellation Centaurus**.

The other Greek Constellations

The other Greek constellations that may be featured one day in a novella include Andromeda, Ara, Auriga, Boötes, Cassiopeia, Cepheus, Corona Australis, Corona Borealis, Corvus, Crater, Delphinus, Equuleus, Eridanus, Lepus, Lupus, Lyra, Pegasus, Perseus, Piscis Austrinus, Triangulum, Ursa Major, Ursa Minor, and Argo Navis (now divided into Carina, Puppis, and Vela)

The stories of these constellations are a watch this space (literally)

Follicle Farm - A novel adventure

Also written by Stephan De Jonghe

Follicle Farm is a comical and imaginative insight into organisational structure and behaviour of the trillions of cells that make up the microscopic world of every living person. It reveals how cells within the human body really think and how they, mostly, work well together. Bobby is a Mitochondria and he works as a humble Follicle Farmer. He, with millions of colleagues, are part of the amazing organisation dedicated to growing hair for the human male that they live inside of. Recently, Bobby made an important discovery when he learned how to reverse the effects of alopecia and greying hair. Now it's up to management to debate if they should use his technique.

Join Bobby as he travels the body, ably assisted by Banjo and Skip, as he meets and deals with other human cells in various systems throughout the body. Bobby quickly learns there is more to management than just servicing the body's needs. Cliques, quirks, politics, unions, and hidden agendas, all thrive in Bobby's world.

You'll share in his adventure of personal growth as he encourages other Follicle Farmers to utilise best practices in growing quality hair.

This book is now available in Paperback or E-Book

Your concise guide to the meaning of life.

Also written by Stephan De Jonghe (non-fiction)

This is a serious book designed to help people. Its main purpose is to assist you on how to gain insights on how to live a happier and more fulfilled life. It will give the you, the reader, instant benefits. It is peppered with many great quotes, many of them are my own. I've combined my interest in philosophy, sociology, psychology, and history to delve into the true meaning of life. The reader will not only understand why they are here, but how to make their experience more meaningful.

My main aim is to inspire readers into taking more control of how they make decisions that positively affect their achievements, successes, happiness, and therefore their well being. The book is a summary of concise points that are easy to learn and apply to the readers life for an immediate benefit. It includes popular relevant quotes to re-enforce the messages and teaching. I have also included personal anecdotes that give real life and meaningful examples of how the material applies to all readers.

Topics include

- an explanation the main purpose for living.
- how to improve your relationships.
- how communication works and how to make it more effective.
- understanding your needs and desires and how to improve outcomes for yourself.
- understanding what motivates other people.
- how to exceed your own expectations.
- understanding your own personal legal, moral, ethical, and value system.
- improving your control over your emotions.
- understanding the concepts of faith, fate and fairness.
- and being better prepared for the final stages of your life.

This book is now available in Paperback or E-Book